It was all right now.

He walked back to the bed. He adjusted the
covers around the girl's neck to hide the bruises.
He stepped back, looked at her again, and nodded.
He picked up his bag and left the room.

The Beast was quiet again.

KATIE'S TERROR

DAVID E. FISHER

CHARTER BOOKS, NEW YORK

This Charter Book contains the complete
text of the original hardcover edition.

KATIE'S TERROR

A Charter Book / published by arrangement with
William Morrow and Company, Inc.

PRINTING HISTORY
William Morrow edition / 1982
Charter edition / February 1984

ISBN: 0-441-43126-7

Charter Books are published by The Berkley Publishing Group,
200 Madison Avenue, New York, N.Y. 10016.
PRINTED IN THE UNITED STATES OF AMERICA

To Ron,
for graduation

CONTENTS

KATIE'S TERROR

PART ONE

THE BEAST
AT MORN

CHAPTER

1

He woke up feeling happy, relaxed, washed clean. He came out of sleep with no movement except for the sudden opening of his eyes. He stared at the ceiling and took pleasure in the slow, easy rhythm of his breathing. The tightness, the devastating anger were gone.

He stretched. The sun was just slipping over the windowsill into the room. He didn't recognize the room. He tried to remember where he was. He glanced around—and saw the girl.

Funny how you can lie in bed with a girl and not be aware that she's there.

He looked away. He tried to listen for the rhythm of her breathing. He held his own breath. The room was infinitely quiet.

Never mind.

He began to remember last night . . . and then, thank God, it slipped away again. He was always afraid, at first, that he would remember it all.

It was all right now.

He sat up. He didn't look at the girl. He got out of bed and went into the bathroom. When he came out again he was carrying his toothbrush and shaving kit and comb. He packed them in the carryall, took out clean underpants and a shirt. He threw in yesterday's dirty clothes. He looked carefully around the room; he didn't want to leave anything behind.

It was early still. He would skip breakfast and catch the train to the city. He wasn't hungry yet. He picked up his carryall and looked once more around the room, standing at the door.

And there was the girl. He saw her only as part of the room, as part of a stage set. He would leave the room, placing the "Do Not Disturb" sign on the door, and the stage would remain dark.

He surveyed the set. He put down his bag and walked back to the bed. He adjusted the covers higher around the girl's neck, to hide the bruises. He stepped back, looked at her again, and nodded. He picked up his bag and left the room.

He walked down the hall to the elevator, rode to the ground floor, and left the hotel. He blinked in surprise. He was on Eighth Avenue. But that's not possible, he had been in Boston yesterday, he had auditioned for a role at the Playhouse, he had not got it, he had . . . what *had* he done?

He couldn't have come back to the city the previous night. He certainly would have stayed overnight. Boston is a lovely town, he thought as he walked toward Forty-second Street. Yes, it must be a lovely town, because even though he hadn't got the job he felt fine this morning.

He was half a block from the hotel now, and he had forgotten all about it. The girl in the bed no longer existed; she had vanished from his mind like chalk dust wiped clean from a blackboard. He breathed in deeply and his lungs filled easily, he was all right again, and he didn't even want to remember why.

From the *Playbill* notes for the Hudson Theatre Guild's production of *The Courtesy Not To Bleed:*

"PETER ABRANTI *(The Waiter)* is no stranger to these boards, having appeared previously in *Da, Molly,* and *The Admirable Crichton.* A graduate of Yale University, the New York-born actor is a veteran of varied theatrical experience throughout America. He has appeared in leading and supporting roles with repertory theatres in Milwaukee, Louisville, and Atlanta, as well as summer stock on Cape Cod. In New York he has been seen Off Broadway with Liza Minnelli, on the television and movie screens, and has long been a familiar face in the world of commercials. He was most recently seen on Broadway in *The Sister."*

A rather impressive résumé. But of course it is difficult to encapsulate a man in one paragraph. Difficult to reach the intricacies of his nature, the subtleties of his varied motivations. There is, in fact, much more to be said about Peter. About the man, about the actor, and about the thing inside struggling to get out.

The beast inside. It had first come to the surface, taking him by surprise, five years ago in Milwaukee, where he had been playing Biff, the son, in *Death of a Salesman.* He hadn't even known it had been there until one night at the end of the run when he had let himself be picked up by one of the groupies at a local pizza and beer palace, had gone to bed with her, and had wakened in the morning to find her cold and strangled.

He hadn't known what had happened, and he hadn't wanted to find out. He had dressed and left the place without being seen.

He had so completely forgotten it had ever happened that when it occurred again, two years later in Louisville, he was again taken completely by surprise.

The third time had been barely a year later, on the Cape, where he was actually with a Broadway try-out which never did make it into town. Then less than a year later in Atlanta, which was only a few months ago.

And now here in his own city—that was stupid, careless, indefensible. How could he allow it to happen right here at home?

He blinked.

Allow *what* to happen?

Nothing had happened.

Had it?

He couldn't remember.

The beast inside was quiet, and out here on the surface there was no trace of the deeply festering abcess.

The maid's name was Estrella. She was Puerto Rican, and a very lucky woman, although she didn't yet know how lucky she was. She worked the third and fourth floors of the Howard Johnson's Motor Inn on Fifty-first and Eighth. She got there every morning at seven-thirty, and by eight-thirty she had her cart loaded with fresh linen, towels, and toilet paper and was ready to begin.

She was known to first-time residents of the motor inn as the "Curse of the Third and Fourth floors" because promptly at eight-thirty she knocked, inserted her passkey into the slot, and opened the first door, all in one rapid motion. Second-time residents of the motor inn had learned to place the Do Not Disturb sign on the door handle.

By eleven forty-five she had finished her first round and was ready for her coffee break. Promptly at twelve o'clock she began her second round, taking care of the rooms that had displayed Do Not Disturb signs early in the morning.

Room 353 still had the sign on the door handle, and she passed it by again.

By two o'clock she had finished all the rooms on the third and fourth floors, except for room 353. She went into the stairwell, sat heavily on the top step, and lit a cigarette.

Her husband was out of work. Her eldest son had just graduated from high school and now he was out of work too. She had been a pretty woman when she was her son's age, but now she no longer looked in the mirrors of the rooms she cleaned. When she saw the pretty women on the New York streets she felt envious and mean. The pretty women did not get up every morning at five-thirty and return home every afternoon with a back that hurt, with ugly veins popping out of their legs and out of the backs of their hands.

She finished the cigarette. Now she could either sit in the stairwell and wait for them to wake up or she could leave the room undone and go home. But if she did that, there would be complaints. They would wake up at three o'clock and when they came home from shopping and eating they would be angry because the room had not yet been cleaned. It was not fair that she had to wait while the rich Anglos slept all day.

She went down the hall and knocked on the door. For some reason she respected the late sleepers more than the early risers; she waited a moment, then she knocked again.

She thought resentfully of the pretty women who could afford to sleep late, and then she put her key into the lock and opened the door.

She was about to find out how lucky she was.

The lady was asleep. She called out softly, then loudly, but the lady did not wake up.

She backed out of the room and closed the door.

She thought, To hell with her. She knew these pretty women, the ones she saw coming out onto the streets when she was going to bed because she had to get up at five-thirty the next morning. She thought, Why should I wait for her? I'm going home.

And then she thought again, of how quietly, how still the lady was lying there.

She opened the door again. *"Lady?"* she called.

The detective's name was Wally Gilford. He was thinking, Well, at least there isn't any blood. The poor kid looked almost as if she were asleep. Not quite. There is a definite if subtle difference between a sleeping girl and a dead body. But at least there wasn't any blood.

He shook his head. He used to be no more cynical than the next fellow. He used to be a pretty happy guy. But that was ten years ago.

Never mind. He looked down at the girl and forgot all that now. He didn't like the whole scene. Not one little bit.

Forget the girl herself, never mind her. The whole scene stank. When a girl gets herself murdered in bed, it's supposed to be what they call a crime of passion.

And these are nice, straightforward, easy crimes to solve. You check into the victim's background and you find that she's been married five years and fooling around for two years and you can wrap the case up in a week, maybe two weeks at the most.

He looked around the room. He didn't like it at all. Nothing was out of place. The lamp hadn't been knocked over. The ashtray hadn't been thrown through the window. The bedclothes weren't even rumpled. It didn't even look as if they had made love.

The girl's bag was on the dresser. It had been the first thing the fingerprint squad had dusted, and Wally looked now at the wallet lying open beside it. The girl's name was Sally Forest. She lived on Twelfth Street.

He didn't like it at all. No attempt to hide her identification, no attempt to throw them off the trail. Of course, they'd have found out who she was eventually, but why not try at least to *delay* them?

It looked as if the killer didn't care if they found out who she was and all about her. Now why wouldn't he be worried about that? The only reason Wally could come up with was that the killer knew he wouldn't be found in her background. And that was what Wally didn't like about this whole scene.

If you didn't kill someone because you were emotionally involved with her, you killed because you wanted her money. But here was the girl's wallet, and there was more than three hundred dollars in it.

If you weren't emotionally involved with a girl, and you didn't want her money, why would you kill her?

Oh thank you, Jesus, Wally thought, thank you a whole fucking heap. Not a psycho, he thought, please God let there be some other explanation. If there is anything we do not need in this city it's a Boston

Strangler. A Jack the Ripper. A Son of goddamn Sam. Come on, Jesus, he begged, let it be something else.

He watched while the squad dusted the room for prints. Usually there weren't any prints. Today there would be too many. There would be prints of the last two dozen occupants of this room, all smeared on top of one another, all unidentifiable.

There would be other clues. A registration card at the front desk, but certainly with a phony name. He looked again around the neat room. Nothing out of place. No, this murder had not been born of a sudden quarrel, an emotional outburst. Nothing in the room was disturbed. Not even the bedclothes. This murder had been done calmly and deliberately.

The name would be phony.

There would be descriptions—from the bellboy, the clerk, the girl at the newsstand. They would remember different people, they would get everyone mixed up. He had been a cop long enough to know. He would interview them all, and then go looking for a short fat thin tall man, blond with black hair and of average height, average weight, average age.

Wally is forty-seven years old. He is one of the smartest and most experienced detectives still investigating scenes-of-crime in New York. He should have been promoted off the streets by now. He should be a lieutenant or even a captain, sitting behind a desk and giving orders to green young detectives. But there is no way to get promoted beyond sergeant in this department without sitting for the lieutenant's exam, and he has refused to sign up for it. Wally is an unusual cop.

For one thing, he is a college graduate. He went to CCNY, in the days before open admissions, when the degree meant something. Although this does not make him unique in the department, it does make him unusual.

For another thing, there is the depth of his feeling about murders like this one. At one time, like most cops, he came to terms with such things. Being a cop was a job like other jobs, like selling insurance. You had to treat it like that or go crazy. You didn't get involved. But that was ten years ago, before his wife—

Never mind that now. Mustn't get involved, must keep the mind clear and analytical.

He thought of his daughter, twenty-four years old, a grad student in sociology at the University of Massachusetts. Or a waitress. She is a great constraint to him; each year as she gets older he finds that he cannot lust after girls her age or younger. Year by year she is wiping out his fantasies. He smiles whenever he thinks of her.

He stops smiling now, looking down at the girl's body. She could be twenty-four years old. She could be a sociology student at the University of Massachusetts. Or a waitress. Or a hooker. She could be anything—no. She *could* have been anything. Now she's nothing.

Well, he thinks again, at least there isn't any blood. Thank you, Jesus, for that.

CHAPTER

2

Katie McGregor Townsend saw him come into the room. He stopped in the doorway, looked around for her, found her, smiled. She smiled back and gestured hopelessly over the bent head of the dark student in front of her. Peter nodded and sat down to wait.

Katie was at the information desk in the main reading room, and the student was an Iranian who could not seem to understand why a book listed as being in the Fifty-second Street annex was not actually in the stacks here in the Forty-second Street library. She finally managed to convince him that it would be necessary to visit the annex, and before anyone else could approach her she left the desk and came across the wide floor to him.

"Haven't I seen you in the movies?" she asked.

"Probably, I went to the movies just last night." She sat beside him and kissed him lightly and he asked, in a thick Brooklyn accent, "Hey, what's a gorgeous sexy lady like you doing in a library, fa Christ's sake? Ya stick with me, kid, and your name'll be up there in lights—"

"Did you get the job?" she interrupted.

"Job?" he asked in his normal voice. "What job?"

"The job you went to Boston for."

"Oh, *that* job." He shrugged. "I didn't really want it. Tiny stage, rotten acoustics. Logan's a good director, but you know how it is with a new play, they've got the lousy playwright sitting in on auditions—"

"Bad vibes, huh?"

"Terrible. You could vomit. They ought to lock playwrights out of the theater until two weeks after opening—they know *nothing* about acting." He paused. "Logan liked me."

"But the playwright—"

"A creep. He wrote the play about his brother or somebody and all he knows is I don't look like the guy he wrote about. What goddamn difference does that make, for Christ's sake? The audience doesn't know his brother—"

"Never mind."

"Yeah. Right. I didn't want the lousy job anyway, not with that creep of a playwright hanging around, breathing over everybody's shoulder during rehearsal. I feel sorry for whoever gets the job." He smiled suddenly. "Well look, what can I tell you? That's show biz, right?"

"That is show biz," she agreed firmly. "That is *exactly* what show biz is."

"Hey, don't knock it. It's all we've got—"

"It may be all *you've* got—"

He kissed her quickly on the cheek and got up. He

didn't want to start that discussion again, not here in public where he couldn't stop her by grabbing her or kissing her or spanking her or *something*. "Dinner tonight, your place?"

"Aren't you working tonight?"

"Monday. Restaurant's closed."

The quick suspicion on her face fled. She was always afraid that he would quit or get fired because he spent so much time going to auditions. She had forgotten it was Monday. She smiled and nodded. "Dinner tonight. My place."

To Whom It May Concern:

It is a distinct pleasure to write this letter of recommendation for Katherine McGregor Townsend, who has been my student for the past three years while obtaining the degree of Master of Library Science.

When I first met Ms. Townsend, I did not expect her to last through the program. She came as a part-time student, thirty-five years old. She had been out of college for nearly fifteen years, working as an actress. She is the kind of person whom you turn your head to look at if you see her on the street, and you say, "She must be an actress." Not flashily beautiful, but strikingly attractive. I never thought she would settle down into our rigorous MLS program.

But she did. She is intelligent as well as lovely. Evidently she was not quite lovely enough—or, more probably, not quite lucky enough—to make a career as an actress, but she is certainly intelligent enough to make one as a librarian. I would rank her in the top fifteen percent of all students I have had in the past ten years.

One final word must be addressed to her enthusiasm for the subject of library science. I mentioned above that she started as a part-time student; she was obviously not committed at that time to a career in libraries, she was searching to find herself. And find herself she did. It has been one of the most rewarding experiences of my teaching career to see her awaken to the beauties of the library system. It has more generally been my experience that students come in with enthusiasm and leave with boredom. But above and beyond the mechanics of library science, Ms. Townsend has come alive to the joy of being surrounded with the greatest books and the greatest words recorded throughout mankind's climb to semi-civilization.

She is a lovely woman, an intelligent person, and an enthusiastic librarian. I heartily recommend her.

Respectfully,

James Caroll
Professor of Library Science

Morning.

Katie's right eye flipped open. She glanced quickly around the room. Nearly eight-fifteen. She rubbed her left eye and it opened. She stretched, took a deep breath. She was awake.

She got out of bed and slipped into her robe. She stood at the foot of the bed, looking down at Peter as she tied the sash and brushed back her hair. She was still warm with sleep and compassion.

She smiled sadly. He didn't sleep here often anymore. Well, he worked late at the Café du Mille and she was long asleep by the time he—no, let's not slip off into excuses. He didn't often stay overnight because she didn't want him to. She looked down at him, her head tilted to one side in thought, and wondered why. She loved him, of course, but she supposed she simply needed her privacy.

She glanced again at the clock and hurried off into the kitchen. Today was the big day; she found herself tingling with excitement despite herself. It was so silly. Ten years ago she would have given her eyeteeth for a chance to be seen on television, but today it was just a giggle. Exciting, of course, but really just a giggle.

It wasn't that she didn't love him, she told herself as she broke the eggs. Clearly she loved him or she wouldn't still be sleeping with him. It was just that she needed the security of her own pad.

Security is something that some people manage to find in marriage, she argued. But no, that was silly. No one would think of marriage to Peter as involving security. No one could find security in marriage to any actor.

Oh, she was well out of that business. Even if she had succeeded, it would have been no good. Success on the stage is remarkably like failure in any other business. She thought of her few friends who *had* succeeded. Success meant frequent three-month stints with the rep groups in Milwaukee or Cleveland or New Haven, with the Arena Stage in Washington or the Taper Forum in Los Angeles or ACT in Seattle or, holy of holies, the Guthrie in godawful Minnesota. And maybe once in a while an Off Broadway role. And if you really reached the pinnacle, a part in a hit play, which meant playing the same role night in and night out until you were walking through it in your sleep.

The only way to break out of the rut would be television, but first she'd rather sell her soul to the devil and all his hordes, or the movies—which meant giving up New York and starting all over again in wonderland-on-the-coast. No thank you.

It was easier for men. Peter lived in daily hope of landing *the* role, the one that would catapult him to stardom. But nobody wrote roles like that for women, nobody since Noel Coward or Tennessee. Why is it that only gay playwrights can write roles for women? Why can't normal playwrights? Why can't *women* write roles for women?

It was funny how things worked out. She hadn't really ever meant to leave the theater, she had gone back to school part-time at first, just to have something to do. And she had discovered a whole new world. And here she was, in just—she glanced at the kitchen clock—in just five minutes about to make her television debut. She poured the coffee and ladled the eggs onto a couple of dishes and put them on the tray.

Peter was still asleep. He didn't seem excited at all. She wondered if he had forgotten. It would be just like him. If *he* wasn't going to be on television, it just didn't exist. She wondered if she would marry him. How does anyone know if she should marry someone?

Stupid question. You should just wake up one morning in a frenzy of passion and run off to the church without even thinking about it.

She sighed. She wasn't going to wake up in any more frenzies of passion. That would be too much to expect, after all. She was nearly forty years old. She could be standing here with the breakfast tray in her hands, looking down on her husband and thinking about their twentieth wedding anniversary, couldn't she? You didn't wake up in a frenzy of passion after being married for twenty years, did you?

The digital clock clicked to 8:58.

She put the tray on the floor beside the bed and grabbed Peter by both shoulders and shook him until his eyes blinked open, then hurried over and turned on the television. He sat up and she got into bed beside him and they settled the tray between them.

"Television?" he asked.

She looked at him. "You forgot," she said.

He looked blank, then suddenly his eyes cleared. "Today?" he asked.

She nodded.

The television screen lit up. The words *Morning in America* came on, in large diagonal letters. She wished she had a color set.

"Did you put sugar in the coffee?" Peter asked.

"Ssshh," she said. Then, "Oh, my God, is that me? I'm beautiful! I'd forgotten what they can do for you with proper makeup . . . oh no! Oh, God, no close-ups!"

"There's no sugar in this coffee."

"*Please,* God, make them move the camera back just a *little.*"

"You look great. You're a beautiful woman, you know that? You make lousy coffee, but you're a beautiful woman."

She grimaced. "I don't look eighteen years old."

"Nobody does. Even nineteen-year-olds don't look eighteen years old."

"Ssshh."

"—and Miss Townsend," the man on the screen was saying, "who looks like your perfectly normal every-day librarian—if your local library board has managed to hire Bo Derek (APPRECIATIVE STUDIO LAUGHTER,

APPLAUSE). Miss Townsend actually has a rather fascinating hobby which she is going to tell us about. Perhaps I shouldn't say *hobby*. What she does is a bit strong for that word. Perhaps I should say *avocation*."

"No," Katie-on-the-screen replied, "*avocation* is much too grand a word. *Hobby* sounds just about right."

The gentleman smiled at her humility, and confided to the audience, "When a young lady's *hobby* is fighting crime, and she does so more effectively than our beleaguered police forces, perhaps a grander word than *hobby* is justified, wouldn't you say? (APPLAUSE) And Miss Townsend will be telling us about her"—he smiled—"*hobby*, right after this."

"Well," Katie said, leaning back against the pillow as two ladies began selling soap on the screen. "That wasn't so bad."

"It wasn't exactly inspirational," Peter said.

"What did you expect? The sleep-walking scene from Macbeth?"

"Don't get upset. That's all I meant, it *isn't* Shakespeare. It isn't *any*thing, is it? It's just you talking about your hobby, right?"

She shrugged. They watched the rest of the commercial in silence. "My *avocation*," she said.

"There's no sugar in this coffee."

"Sshh, they're starting."

"Miss Townsend, before you tell us how you use the unique resources of the New York Public Library in your personal battle against crime, I think perhaps our audience would like to know something about you as a person. Could you tell us about your background? You began life here in New York City as an actress, didn't you?"

"Yes. Well, actually, I began life in Toledo, Ohio. As

a baby. I majored in drama at Kenyon College and came to New York to be an actress."

"I would think you'd be a very successful actress. You seem to have all the attributes. You're certainly not nervous here in front of an audience, you've got a friendly, relaxed manner, and you're quite lovely—"

"There's a bit more to it than that, as I quickly discovered. No, that's not right. I didn't discover it quickly. It took years and years, believe me."

"Years of making the rounds? Unsuccessfully?"

She nodded. "I got off the bus with a thick scrapbook full of pictures and reviews of our college productions—we had done it all, I had played Masha in *Three Sisters*, Laura in *Menagerie*, the usual assortment in *Milkwood*—and I found out that nobody in the big city had heard or *cared* about Kenyon College. I spent the next fifteen years here, battering my thick head against even thicker wooden doors that never opened. I'd get an occasional audition, more occasionally—or less occasionally, I guess I mean—I'd get a callback. A couple of times I even got a small role Off Off Broadway. Both times I thought that was *it*, I was on my way. On my way to the unemployment office, it turned out. That's success in this business, you know."

"The unemployment office?"

Katie nodded. "That's the criterion. If you make enough money in any six-month period to qualify for unemployment as an out-of-work actress, you're considered a professional. And that's *success*, compared to the kids from Kenyon College and Texas A and M and Purdue and wherever who are still wandering the streets trying to make a buck. Is that crazy? I mean, is that nuts?"

"It's certainly not an easy life."

"It's a *crazy* life. I woke up one morning and asked myself, What am I doing? Working in a profession where the height of success—I mean that you can reasonably expect—is to qualify for unemployment! I just asked myself what future I had. And the answer was, none. That's a pretty sobering thought, you know."

"I guess we've all had mornings when we wake up like that."

"But that's just depression. This was *true*. So I just asked myself what I'd *rather* be doing. And the answer astonished me."

"You had never thought about being a librarian before?"

"I always liked libraries, but I never thought about it as a career. I guess I just took them for granted. Like, when I came here to New York, the first place I ever hung around was the main library on Forty-second Street. I mean, I just naturally gravitated there. I felt at home. And so that day when I woke up and asked myself all these questions—the day of my Great Awakening, I still think of it—I simply got up and got dressed and took the subway down to the admissions office of City University and told them I wanted to start work on an MLS."

"That's a Master of Library Science degree?"

"Right. I studied part-time, because I wasn't committed right away. In my own mind, I mean. But as soon as I started, I knew that was what I wanted."

"And you completed the degree . . . when?"

"Just last year. It took me three years."

"And now you're working at the main library?"

"Yes. Can you imagine the luck? I mean, that's

librarian heaven, the big league. It's not much of a job, of course, I just fill in all over the place, but actually that's just great. I'm learning all the jobs, circulation and cataloging and interlibrary loan and serials—"

"And you have all the resources of that great library—one of the finest in the world, I understand—to apply to your crusade against crime."

"Oh, that's just a sort of hobby—"

"Well, we certainly want to hear all about it on our next segment. So stay tuned," he told the camera, "and we'll be right back."

"I'll get us coffee," Peter said, slipping out of bed. "With sugar."

When he returned with two cups, she was staring at the commercial, but you could tell she wasn't seeing it. She looked up at him and smiled. "What do you think?" she asked.

He handed her the cups and slipped back into bed, sipped his coffee and stared down into it. He shook his head. "You're doing it all wrong," he said.

"I'm doing *what* all wrong? I thought I was pretty good."

"Good?"

"Well, you know, interesting? I didn't stutter and I didn't repeat myself too badly, and I looked great—if I were rich, I'd hire that makeup girl away from NBC. Maybe we could kidnap her?"

"You know what I mean," he said.

"No, I don't. What do you mean?"

"Look, being a librarian is good, being smart is good—"

"Thank you very much—"

"—but you have to play it right."

"*Play* it—"

"This business about the mysterious masked lady of the night who combats the denizens of the underworld in her never-ending battle against crime, that's all fine, but you're wasting it."

"I don't know what you're talking about."

"What's the whole point of this whole business?"

"What business? What point?"

"Damn it, you make me mad sometimes! Look, you've got national exposure here, right? People are going to be interested. But instead of playing it like an intelligent actress who manages the New York Public Library system in her spare time and captures desperate criminals on her coffee break, you're coming on as just another girl from Ohio who wanted to be an actress, and who now really *is* a librarian."

"I *am* a librarian!"

"You're an actress! You're *working* as a librarian—"

"No!" She faced him in the bed. "No, Peter, I *used* to be an actress. Now I'm a librarian. I *want* to be a librarian."

"You still go out on auditions—"

"No."

"You do! Remember that last call I got for you?"

"That was six months ago and I didn't get the job and I didn't even *want* the job, I only went to please you and I knew I wasn't going to get it and I *didn't* get it."

"That's *why* you didn't get it! You have to *know* you're going to get it—"

"Like you knew about this job in Boston?"

He recoiled, spilling the coffee. Immediately she reached out, touched him. "I'm sorry."

He took a drink of the coffee.

How could she explain to him? People grow up.

Eventually even actresses. Can't actors? Can't he understand that she has found another career, one that she likes, one that she can handle, where she can make a contribution? Can't he understand that it's time he grew up, too?

"You're missing the program," he said, gesturing with his shoulder toward the screen.

"Oh, fuck the program!" she said. "We have to talk!"

"Ssshh," he said, not looking at her, nodding again at the screen, hiding from her in its glare.

She folded her arms across her chest and pushed herself angrily back into the pillows. He would never talk about it. He was a good actor, she supposed—hell, she didn't know if he was or not, she didn't know what was good anymore. All she knew was, you couldn't make a living in the theater.

She did know he was more than just a good waiter; he was a good host. And he had worked at the Café du Mille for long enough to have learned almost everything about the restaurant business. If he would work full-time there—if he would work lunch hours as well as evenings—with the outrageous tips he managed to get and the income tax he managed not to pay, he could save enough in just a couple of years to buy into a small French restaurant. He could have a real human-type existence instead of the actor's fantasy life.

But he wouldn't do it. He wouldn't work lunch hours because he had to be free for casting calls during the day. Never mind that there weren't more than a dozen a year. He simply refused to work lunch hours; he wouldn't even *talk* about it.

She glared at the screen, where Katie was explaining

how sl.e had combined a perfectly ordinary morbid interest in crime with the unique resources of the world's greatest library and had quite unexpectedly come up with the solution to a murder.

"This was four or five months ago," she said, "and I was working in the newspaper room. The library subscribes to newspapers from all over the country. All over the world, really. Part of my job was to keep them in order in the reading room because people read them and it's so easy to mess up a newspaper and most people don't even bother to try to put them back together. People really are slobs, aren't they? It comes from watching too much television, I think. They grow up being used to the whole world just disappearing when they flip off the switch, so there's no need ever to clean anything up."

It suddenly occurred to her that perhaps this wasn't the right time and place to blame the world's ills on television, and she said, "But I suppose that's too much of a simplification. Anyway, you know how it's impossible to straighten out a newspaper, refold it and all, once it gets crumpled? Well, it's even harder to do it without reading it. So there I was, refolding and reading all these newspapers from all over the country, and of course the national and international news is the same everywhere and not so interesting, but the thing that *is* interesting in reading papers from Cleveland and Pittsburgh and Toledo and Santa Fe is the local stories. And of course the most interesting local stories are the murders, aren't they?"

"So you became sort of an expert on the murders going on all over this country, is that it?"

"No, I wouldn't say an expert. But I did read about an awful lot of them. You'd be amazed at how many people get killed every day. At any rate, what happened was that I was reading an article in the San Jose *Mercury-News* about a woman who shot her husband in the middle of the night. He had been out drinking with some of his friends and she had gone to sleep early.

"Now what she said was that their house had been broken into recently. They had reported a couple of burglaries to the police, and in fact they had been so worried that her husband had bought a gun and they had installed a burglar-alarm system."

"Too complex," Peter said.

"What?" Katie-in-bed asked.

"Sentence structure should be simpler. More direct. Audiences have limited attention spans. By the end of the sentence they've forgotten what the subject noun was. That's why nobody reads Goethe anymore."

He's too smart to be a waiter, Katie thought, that's the problem. Why did his goddamn family ever let him become an actor? Why didn't his mother make him be a neurosurgeon like all the other kids?

Katie-on-the-screen was saying, "So this evening she was sound asleep and suddenly in the middle of the night the burglar alarm went off, ringing and ringing. She jumped up and grabbed the gun because, you see, her husband wasn't home. She sat there in her bed, terrified in the dark, while the alarm bells screamed and then suddenly the bedroom door banged open and the intruder lurched in.

"Well, she couldn't see him, of course, because it was pitch black so she screamed, 'Who is it?' and he didn't answer but he lunged toward her and she was holding the gun in both her hands and she didn't even realize it when it went off and the man fell.

"When she got out of bed and turned on the lights she saw that it was her husband. She called the police and the ambulance but there was nothing they could do. He was dead when they got there."

"That's the sort of thing that might happen anywhere, isn't it?" the host asked. "In fact, that's the kind of story that provides a rationale for the people who argue that we shouldn't—as private citizens—keep handguns around the house."

"Of course," Katie agreed. "That's why she was going to get away with it. It sounded so reasonable. They had been having trouble with burglars, the alarm system was new, the husband had been drinking—the alarm system is one of those types where after you open the door you have to punch out a certain combination of numbers on a wall switch, and he must have gotten mixed up and hit the wrong combination. You only have about thirty seconds to do it, so before he could get it straight the alarm must have gone off.

"Well then, as soon as he heard it ring, he quickly ran upstairs to his bedroom to tell his wife that it was all right, but either he was so drunk that his speech was slurred—although the autopsy didn't show that much alcohol—or maybe she was just so scared that she panicked and shot before he could get the words out.

"She was terribly upset, and the hundred-thousand-dollar insurance policy they had recently taken out only added to the bathos of the scene. Everybody was terribly sympathetic. It was a very plausible story."

"A very plausible story indeed, but"—turning to the camera—"before all you ladies run out to buy a new insurance policy on your husband's life and a new handgun from the corner sporting-goods store, we'd better find out the end of the story. I imagine"—he turned back to Katie—"this is where you come into the picture."

"Well, I read all this in the paper, you see, and it would have sounded as plausible to me as it did to everyone else—I don't have any special powers of detection, nothing like that—but I do have a good memory. All that training as an actress, probably. I was always a quick study."

"Bravo," Peter muttered.

"Sshh," Katie-in-bed said. "It's getting interesting."

"So as soon as I read the story," she said on the screen, "it struck me that I had read something of the sort not too long ago. So I looked over the story again. It mentioned that the insurance policy had only recently been bought, and in fact that the couple were practically newlyweds—they had been married less than three months.

"Well, that was a big help. I had been working in the library only just over six months, so anything that might have happened of a similar nature must have happened within this limited time span. I didn't remember exactly where I had read the similar story, but I had a—oh, a sort of subliminal vision about the kind of paper it had been in, do you know what I mean? I knew it wasn't *The New York Times* or the *Manchester Guardian* or the *Miami Herald* or any big paper like that. It was one of the small-town papers. And of course there are an awful lot of them, and a three-month period is really a long time, but you know it's only a hobby and so it didn't matter how much time it took because that's what a hobby's supposed to do, isn't it? Take up your time?

"So I spent the next several weeks looking through a variety of newspapers. And finally I found it."

"Found what?"

"Another story, in the *St. Augustine Times-Leader*, that was nearly identical. A lady there had recently been married, taken out insurance, been bothered by break-ins and had purchased a handgun and a burglar alarm system. The husband had come home late at night from an evening out with the boys, the alarm system had gone off, and she had killed him."

"The identical story."

"Exactly. And it happened just a few months before the lady in San Jose had gotten married to her soon-to-be-deceased husband. Well, it sounded like a bit too much of a coincidence to me!"

"Yes, I can see where it might! But what did you do about it?"

"I didn't know *what* to do. Do you know what I mean? It all sounded so Jane Marple-ish for me to call up the police and tell them I had found evidence that might turn an accidental death into murder most foul. I was afraid of looking ridiculous."

"Yes, that's a problem we all have. I wonder if that's the reason so many people don't want to get involved when they see something happening on the street. They're afraid it'll turn out to be a husband and wife quarrel, and they don't want to look silly by coming to the woman's rescue."

"I think you're right. But this was obviously something more than just a domestic quarrel, and I felt I had to do something."

"What did you do?"

"Well, I just sat myself down and made the long-distance call to the San Jose police department, and I must say they were very nice about it. I was expecting—well, I don't know what, but all I had ever heard of the police was, like, how they behaved in Chicago in 1968 or how they snarl at you in New York. I mean, I always think of them as 'the fuzz,' or 'the pigs,' but this detective in charge of the case listened to everything I had to say, and he asked if I would send him a Xerox copy of the newspaper article from St. Augustine, and I did, and he got in touch with the police there and they found that although the lady had used a different name there the description of her in both cities matched. And so they flew someone who had known her in St. Augustine out to San Jose and it really was the same person."

"And so you had solved your first crime."

"Well, I didn't think of it in terms of being my *first* crime. I never thought there might be a second."

"But there was a second, wasn't there?"

"Well, yes."

"The same sort of situation? Where you saw the same crime being committed in different cities? Through the library's newspaper collection?"

"No, this was a little different. It started when I was glancing through a human-interest story on the women's page of a small paper in—well, I don't think I should mention the town because the case hasn't gone to trial yet, but the story was about the local doctor whose second wife had just died of unknown but natural causes, as they put it. The article was about how this dedicated doctor, whose life was spent saving people's lives, was helpless to do anything to save the lives of each of his two beloved wives, who simply wasted away and died.

"Now because he was a doctor—that was the point

of the whole article—they went into some detail about the *symptoms*, you see. And this time that's what struck a chord. I knew I had read something about that sort of thing. This time it was easy to remember where, because I don't read a lot of books about poisoning and sickness and things like that. But I had been involved in reshelving the library's collection of the *Annals of the New York Academy of Sciences* and I was glancing through the books as I was putting them away, and they had had a conference recently on human nutrition and what they call trace elements. These are different things in the soil that are either good or bad for you, like chlorine in the drinking water.

"Anyhow, they had a whole meeting about it, and one of the things they discussed was something called selenium. It turns out that a little bit of selenium is good for you, but too much is a deadly poison. And in fact they had shown that a lot of times, when people had simply died for no apparent reason, it was really due to selenium poisoning. These people would have had a well dug on their property for drinking water, and the soil might have been very rich in selenium—it was usually something like that.

"And the other thing that really made me suspicious was they had found that if you had a lot of copper in your diet along with selenium, the two of them bonded chemically so that the selenium didn't hurt you. But if you didn't have all this extra copper, then the selenium was a poison.

"So it seemed right away that anyone who knew this—and remember the husband of these two women who died was a doctor—could put selenium in both their food and then he could take vitamin tablets or minerals or something that had lots of copper, and he'd be all right, but his poor wife would just waste away and die."

"But that wouldn't be called death by natural causes, would it? And you told us that's what the newspaper article said the two wives had died of."

"Oh, but you see nobody ever suspects selenium poisoning because it's so rare. There are maybe one or two cases a year in the whole country. There are no specific symptoms, you don't turn blue and your toes don't curl up or anything like that. What happens is that the selenium combines with the blood so it can't carry oxygen or wastes, and the whole body just slowly deteriorates and dies. And no one would ever suspect selenium is the reason."

"Until you made another long-distance phone call, am I right?"

"Well, yes. I never would have had the courage to do it, except that I had been right the other time, so I did and I don't know why they believed me unless they already suspected something. Anyhow, they dug up the bodies and examined them for traces of selenium, and it was there all right."

"But is that evidence of murder? Is it, I mean, evidence that the husband poisoned them? Couldn't there have been some other source for the selenium?"

"Well, that's the interesting part. Because if there was, if their water was contaminated or something like that, why didn't the husband get sick and die too?"

"I see what you mean. But is that proof? Beyond a reasonable doubt? Maybe, as you say, it was the water that was contaminated and the husband drank nothing but scotch?"

(STUDIO LAUGHTER)

"Where do they get these people?" Peter asked. "Actors out of work all over the country and they hire people like *that*."

"That's what I mean by the interesting part," Katie said on the screen. "The proof hinges on whether or not he has both selenium and copper in his blood. And the only way they can tell that is to test it, and he won't give them a blood sample. His lawyer says it would be self-incrimination and the Fifth Amendment comes into it. So that's what's going on right now, I don't know how it will turn out."

The host turned and smiled at the camera. "What was it that old radio show used to tell us? Life can be beautiful? Well, as you can see from Miss Katie McGregor Townsend, life can certainly be interesting if you keep your eyes open. And as we'll see in a moment, it can be even more interesting if we use not only our eyes, not only our five senses, but our sixth sense as well. Don't go away."

"Now *talk* to me, damn it!" Katie said. "I want to *talk* about it."

He turned his head and stared at her solemnly. Then slowly, without apparent motion—she never knew how he did this—his eyes began to twinkle. And then his mouth spread into a grin, a grin that used to melt her heart. Oh, hell, what could she do? It still did.

"Let us talk then, you and I," he said.

"I want to talk *seriously*—"

"Of ships and seals and kingly wax and whether birds have wings—"

"Of you and me and living in New York City!"

"Oh, that." The smile faded. He shrugged. "What can I tell you? You'll get over it."

"I'll get over *what*?"

"This *mishegoss* about living the contented life as a librarian in suburbia with a hard-working husband who pays income tax and goes bowling with the good ol' boys from the VFW—"

"Oh, that's *so* unfair! All I want—"

"What?" he shouted suddenly. "*What* do you want?"

She stared at him. His sudden anger frightened—no, he couldn't *frighten* her—but his anger unsettled her, disturbed her. She thought for the first time that all this might be even more serious to him than to her.

And she didn't know what to say. She shrugged. "A normal life," she said.

He didn't answer, and she didn't know what else to say. He stared in silence at the screen, watching that disgusting woman soaking women's fingers in detergent and smirking at them, and Katie, too, kept her face turned toward the screen and watched him out of the corner of her eye.

When the commercial finally ended and the show came back on, a white-haired wild-looking woman was sitting next to her up on the screen. No, *wild-looking* was not the appropriate term. Her features, in fact, gave an impression of serenity. But her clothing—not so much in black and white on the small screen, but in living color at the taping as Katie remembered it—was definitely barbaric.

"Madame Szilardi is a self-confessed mystic who, like Miss Townsend, has turned her powers to the detection and punishment of crime—"

"No, no, no," the white-haired lady interrupted. "First of all, I'm a medium, not a mystic. I'm not even sure just exactly what a *mystic* is. Are you?"

"Well no, not exactly, I just assumed—"

"*Never* assume. It makes an ass out of you and me. Don't you see? Oh, don't you? An *ass* out of *you* and *me*. My third-grade teacher used to tell us that. We all got a terrible kick out of it. I've always wanted to be able to say it myself. In public. So, no, I'm a medium, not a mystic. And I haven't turned my powers toward anything, because a medium has no possible control over what comes to her. To use the word *powers* at all is to be quite misleading."

"Well, perhaps you would tell us exactly what you have done, Madame Szilardi."

"Oh dear, I'm afraid I haven't done anything at all, in the sense that you mean. Nothing so brilliant as Miss Townsend's deductions—I've been watching the show on the monitor in the green room, dear, and I must tell you I think you're absolutely marvelous (STUDIO APPLAUSE) and I feel quite embarrassed when this gentleman goes on as if I had done something comparable. And I've done nothing at all, really."

"Perhaps I should tell our audience," the host told the camera directly, "that Madame Szilardi has provided information to the police in several cities pertinent to crimes that had been unsolved. For example, in Houston she was responsible for the apprehension of a multiple rapist-murderer who had been terrorizing the community for years."

"Oh, I wouldn't say that, really I wouldn't. No, I'm sure you're going rather too far. Actually I did no more than any decent citizen would do when certain facts became known to me. I simply communicated these facts to the police."

"And what were the facts, and how did they become known to you?"

"I didn't ferret them out, if that's what you mean. I did tell that lovely young lady of yours—the one who interviewed me—that I simply wasn't able to say that I went flying through the night on a broom handle or consulted with spirits and cacadaemons. I *did* explain all this to her, you know."

"We wouldn't want you to tell us anything more than what is strictly true. But all you're telling us is what you *didn't* do. What is it that you *did* do?"

"Well then, so long as we understand each other, because, you know I've always been quite strict about not making extravagant claims. I did nothing more than tell the police in Houston what poor Jane Wilshire told me."

"Jane Wilshire being one of the victims, is that right?"

"Yes, exactly. She didn't know exactly who the man was, you understand, but she was able to give a very accurate description and I simply passed that on to the police."

"And why didn't Jane go directly to the police?"

"Well, that would have been a bit difficult, don't you see?"

"Why?"

"Well, she was dead, wasn't she?"

"Dead."

"Yes. Oh, I see. Is that the point you were trying to make? Oh yes, she was quite dead. But that's the whole *point* of a medium, isn't it? There's nothing particularly unusual about it. A *medium* is simply a medium through whom communication may take place."

"So Jane Wilshire, a murdered victim, described her assailant to you. Is that right?"

"And I simply passed the information on to the police. I wasn't responsible for ferreting it out, you see, as dear Miss Townsend did."

"And I believe another of your cases was even more spectacular?"

"No."

The host stared at her, nonplussed for a moment.

Madame Szilardi shrugged. "I suppose what I mean is that I wish you wouldn't use that word spectacular. It's the sort of thing the *National Enquirer* says. It's precisely why I won't talk to them anymore."

"Do you mean," Katie asked, "that you really don't think it's anything at all spectacular to communicate with—spirits?"

"Oh dear," Madame said, leaning forward and taking Katie's hand, "I suppose you're right. I have to admit that it's at least unusual. In the sense that most people can't quite manage it. But the connotations of the word appall me, don't you see?"

"Of course I do. I think you're quite right to discourage that sort of talk."

"Thank you, my dear. You *are* a love, aren't you? I knew from the first moment I saw you on the monitor that we should get along famously."

"Madame Szilardi," the host interrupted, "I've been trying to think of some other word we might use to describe your other case, and I can't come up with one. I'm afraid it's nothing short of spectacular."

"Oh," she said to Katie, "he's probably talking about that terrible ax murder. Now I really do not understand why people persist in referring to it as more spectacular; it's all much of a muchness, surely."

"Certainly there are similarities. It is true, for

ınstance, that again in this case you were told details of the crime and the criminal by the dead victim—"

"Oh, poor Daphne, a very sweet girl. I still do not understand how she managed to get herself mixed up with that terrible man. But that is so often the way of the world, isn't it? A well-brought-up young lady, whom you'd think would associate only with Princeton boys, is attracted instead to the brutes of this world. Oh, I tell you, there are times when I'm glad I was never fortunate enough to become a mother. Not, of course, when I see a lovely young lady like you," she said to Katie, still patting her hand.

"Thank you," Katie smiled.

"The spectacular aspect of this particular case—" the host pushed on "—if anything can be said to be *more* spectacular than the simple fact of a dead person communicating with the living—"

"We don't like to use the word *dead*, you know," Madame Szilardi interrupted. "It's so undescriptive, isn't it? Or rather, erroneously descriptive. It describes the empty body left behind in the coffin, but surely not the spirit soaring free, whose existence is not cut short nor even curtailed but only, shall we say, *shifted* into another dimension."

"At any rate," the harried host rushed on, "the spectacular aspect of the particular case I am referring to is that the victim was not only murdered but also chopped up into little pieces, isn't that so?"

"I'm afraid that's all too true."

"And those pieces were dispersed from New York as far as Wyoming. Sent by parcel post, weren't they?"

Madame Szilardi nodded. "That dreadful man hoped to confuse the various law-enforcement agencies as to who should have jurisdiction over the case. Luckily poor Daphne spoke up and I was able to tell the police exactly where the murder took place."

"And where was that?"

"Right here in Manhattan. Not five blocks from where we are right now. And, indeed, when they looked at the location they found indisputable evidence of the event, in the form of blood and bits of skin and the like. Such tiny little specks they are able to work with! Really miraculous, don't you think? But I do hope," she said suddenly and severely, "that you weren't referring to the case as spectacular simply because poor Daphne was dismembered?"

"Well, granted that communication with the—if not *dead*, then at least *departed*—is possible at all, it does seem that it might perhaps be more difficult to communicate with only *part* of the departed, so to speak?"

(STUDIO LAUGHTER)

"Oh, I am suprised at you! Really, I *am*. The fact of bodily dismemberment does not in any way imply *spiritual* dismemberment. How could one possibly dismember a spirit? Really, that is most unworthy of you."

"I am sorry, Madame Szilardi. I see now how silly that was. I hope you'll forgive me?"

"We'll say no more about it."

"To change the subject, perhaps you two ladies could tell us what cases you are working on at the moment?"

"Oh no," Madame Szilardi said. "Not possibly."

"But why not?"

"The case I am currently involved with is one whose details I am sure should not be discussed in public, particularly on the television—which small children might be watching. No, it's quite out of the question."

"Surely it couldn't be more gruesome than the two cases you have already discussed with us?"

"My dear sir, if I were to tell you of the evil that exists in this world, you would be positively shocked. We'll say not another word, if you please."

"Miss Townsend, then—?"

"Well, I'm in the same situation, though for a different reason. I *am* working on something, but it would be premature to discuss it."

"Just a hint or two?"

"Well, it's basically the same thing as my first case. I've come across several murders in different cities that seem to be related. It's much more difficult to tell this time, because they're the sort of things that might be simple muggings or robberies, and yet they all seem to have some subtle aspects in common. I don't think I should say any more."

"But how will you track down the killer in such a situation?"

"What I'm looking for," she answered reluctantly, "is to see if there are any other things happening in each of those cities at just those times. Suppose I found by checking the entertainment sections of the newspapers that the New York Philharmonic had been playing in each of those cities at just the times that the murders were committed. Then one might begin to suspect that there was a connection, do you see? Of course, I'm just making that up about the New York Philharmonic; I don't for a moment suspect one of them."

"But the killer could be anyone. He could be with the Philharmonic or the circus, he could be a traveling salesman or an itinerant peddler—"

"Exactly. So you can see I don't expect any quick results. It would be an impossible problem for the police, who have so much work to do. But for a simple librarian with a hobby, time isn't so important."

Terror.
Destruction.
Fear.
The commercial came on and Peter stared at it fixedly, but did not see it.

Somewhere in his mind a switch had clicked, and he was gone, lost in fear.

His mind was somewhere between the television set and the bed. He was someone between Peter and the thing inside bursting to get out.

His eyes stared at the set, following with intense concentration the inane words that flickered across the screen: . . . *deodorant* . . . *safety* . . . *dry* . . . *safety* . . . *safety* . . .

There was no safety.

He couldn't think—he couldn't allow his mind to think. And so his conscious mind read the words religiously, and his unconscious mind ran amok.

What had she said? Trace a killer? A killer who struck in different cities! The cases all similar. . . . Searching for some event *or some person* common to each city at the time of each murder . . .

She was on his trail!

His conscious mind saw only the deodorant commercial on the television screen, his subconscious mind saw only Katie beside him in the bed.

Katie kept her face turned fixedly toward the screen, but was looking at him out of the corner of her eye. She wondered what he was thinking. Was he angry? It had been the wrong time to bring up the subject of his quitting show business and working full time at the restaurant, with her up there on the television screen. Of course he was angry! She knew how he must envy her. He could have turned exposure like this into the break he was looking for. Why had it happened instead to her? Oh, Lord, why didn't she ever have the sense to keep her mouth shut at the proper time?

And Peter stared at the set, concentrating on the words there, struggling to hold down the beast inside, unable to allow himself to be aware of the struggle that was taking place.

He was very tired.

His hands, clenched together under the covers, relaxed.

His right hand, moving of its own volition, unknown to his conscious mind, which still listened to the droning television commercial, slid itself loose from the constricting fingers of the left hand and moved up across his chest, out from under the covers.

It rested there for a moment, free again.

He turned his head toward Katie. And smiled.

Katie, surreptitiously watching him, relaxed with a sigh. He was smiling again. She turned her face to him and smiled. She kissed him tenderly on the nose and turned back to the set as the commercial ended.

The right hand moved. It inched lightly across the covers, came to rest on Katie's shoulder.

She reached up to it, touched it, rubbed her fingers gently against the soft hairs on its back.

It moved across her shoulder, caressed her collarbone, rested its own fingers on her soft throat. Like a spider it waited there, paused . . .

The program had entered its closing moments. The host was thanking Katie and Madame Szilardi.

Katie-in-bed smiled with the spider at her throat as Katie-on-the-screen and Madame Szilardi held hands and smiled and said loving things to each other. The old lady really was a dear, the sweetest thing—but wait, here it came now, the strangest thing. Katie wondered if the camera would catch it—yes, the camera was just beginning to pan away from the two women when a sudden, violent spasm of alarm spread across Madame Szilardi's face. The camera paused for an instant, uncertain what to do, then zoomed back onto her.

And the spider fingers encircled her throat. She didn't notice. She was leaning forward slightly now, intent on the screen. It had happened so quickly at the time, she hadn't quite been sure what Madame Szilardi had meant.

Peter lay next to her, intent only on her and on the fingers around her throat, helpless to stop them.

"Is something wrong, Madame Szilardi?" the host asked.

She looked around wildly, then a queer divergence occurred. The lower half of her face, her mouth, smiled abashedly and self-consciously, apologetically. The upper half, the eyes, still glanced frightened in all directions as if fearing—what?

"No," she said. "I'm so sorry."

"Are you feeling all right?"

"Oh yes, it's nothing like that. It's just that—sometimes, I get these . . . sensations? Intimations? I don't know what to call them. I was suddenly afraid that something terrible was happening."

"Happening where? To whom?"

"I don't know! To one of us." She put her hand protectively on Katie's shoulder, looked around the studio. "But nothing is happening, is it?"

"I think we're all safe enough, if that's what you mean."

"But I don't *know* what I mean! Oh I'm sorry, I'm being silly, it was just . . . well, never mind. I must have been wrong."

"Is it all right now?" Katie-on-the-screen asked.

In bed, the fingers around her throat began to tighten. Not quite noticing, only subliminally aware of the discomfort, Katie-in-bed raised her own hands to them but kept staring at the screen.

Madame Szilardi's eyes still darted anxiously, looking in vain for the danger. Her mouth said, "I'm sorry to be such a nuisance. But I have this terrible feeling something is happening to one of us—"

"A premonition of danger?" the host asked, almost forgetting to smile.

"You don't understand! Something is happening right *now*." She stopped, paused, looked around. "At least, that's what I thought, what I *felt*. But that's silly, isn't it? We're all here, and safe, and nothing is happening, is it?"

"We're all quite safe," the host assured her. "And nothing at all is happening."

Katie-in-bed suddenly gasped. The fingers had tightened, they were clasped around her throat, she couldn't—she twisted hard, and pulled at them. "Peter," she gasped, "I can't breathe!"

She clutched at the fingers, she twisted and turned toward Peter and saw suddenly in his eyes staring at her an awful frightening terror. She didn't understand it, but instinctively she let go of the fingers and threw her arms around him. "Peter, I'm so sorry!"

The fingers loosened with her movement. They

hung on as she fell across him.

"Never mind, it doesn't matter," she soothed him. What a bitch she was, how unsympathetic she had been! She shouldn't have been nagging him about his restaurant job at the same time that she herself was on television. How cruel she had been, how unthinking.

Her arms folded around him, and the fingers fell away from her throat.

He blinked. It was gone.

He couldn't even remember what had nearly happened. He almost had it on the tip of his memory. Thank God it was gone!

It must have been a waking nightmare. He was here in bed with Katie now, safe with her arms around him and her lips on his face.

There was no danger, there was only love.

He had to believe that.

On the screen Madame Szilardi said, "I'm sorry to have made such a fool of myself. It *is* more of an art than a science, don't you see? One can't always be quite sure."

"Don't apologize," the host said. "It was a fascinating experience for us to catch even this slight glimpse into the interaction of our world with that other one. You're sure you're all right now?"

"Oh, yes. It's quite all right now."

In bed it was quite definitely all right now. Whatever had happened, Peter no longer remembered. Katie was smothering him now with her weight, a glorious asphyxiation. He rolled over on top of her—

The phone rang.

He looked down at her.

She looked up at him. "It's probably someone calling about the program," she said.

He nodded. "The adulation of the masses," he said. "Such a bother."

She smiled. "I'd better answer, and then take the phone off the hook."

He nodded and lay back in the bed. Katie hopped out and picked up the phone. "Madame Szilardi!" she called out in surprise. "Did you see the program?"

"Dear child," Madame talked breathlessly, "I was watching it and suddenly got the funniest feeling! I don't mean funny, I mean—"

"Yes, I know. Strange."

"The strangest feeling. At the very end, don't you see, when I was frightened?"

"Yes."

"Afraid that something terrible was happening?"

"Yes."

"To one of us?"

"Yes."

"But don't you see?" she cried. "Nothing terrible was happening!"

"That's nothing to be upset about. You were simply mistaken—"

"No, no, you don't understand! I realized just now that something terrible was happening not when we *taped* the show, but when the show was *shown*!"

"Oh."

"So I thought I had better call."

"That's so sweet of you."

"Then you *are* all right?"

"Perfectly."

"Nothing terrible happened?"

"Nothing at all. I'm quite safe, here with my best friend."

"Oh." A long pause. "You're absolutely sure about

that, I suppose? Well, never mind. I'm so glad you're
safe—"

Katie nearly laughed at the disappointment in her
voice.

"—and I won't keep you any longer. I'm sure you've
things to do."

"Yes, as a matter of fact, I was just in the middle of
something."

"It *is* more of an art than a science, you see," she
added apologetically.

"I do see. And perhaps we could meet for coffee
sometime?"

Madame Szilardi's voice brightened again. "I *would*
like that. I'll ring off now, and you get back to
whatever you were doing."

"I'll do that," Katie promised, and they hung up, and
she turned back to her best friend and put her arms
around him and they got back to whatever they had
been doing.

CHAPTER

3

Maybe this is the way people are supposed to behave. Maybe it's me that's crazy, Detective Sergeant Wally Gilford thought.

But he didn't really think so. He sat at his desk in the police station and looked over the report he had just typed, summarizing his investigation into the death of the girl in the Howard Johnson's two days ago.

The two-day mark was an important juncture in this kind of investigation. If no leads surfaced in these first two days, it was a good bet the whole shebang would end in the dead file.

He looked down at the report, then out the window. He had a better view from this report than from that window of what life in the city was really like. And he didn't like the view at all.

I don't know, he thought again, maybe I'm the crazy one.

It was a comforting thought. It would feel more secure to be crazy than to live in a world where men pick up pretty young women and take them to bed and murder them.

For no reason whatsoever.

The girl's name was Sally Forest. She was twenty years old. Had been twenty years old. Her family lived in Jersey, God help them. She had come to New York last year to be an actress, like all the hordes of them, lemmings all, and like them all with no hope of success. She had never acted anywhere. She had no idea of what was involved beyond the concept they all seemed to have: pretty girls in beautiful dresses on the TV or the movie screen. Why can't their parents keep them safe in Jersey?

According to her friends, the reality she had discovered on the streets hadn't seemed to bother her. Being an actress was the excuse she had given her family, but being free and alone in New York was the *reason* she had come.

She had taken full advantage of the city. She had been what he had always dreamed of finding when he was a teen-ager, a pretty girl who was free and promiscuous to the point of casualness. And so she had last been seen two nights ago in Mcsorley's, being chatted up by a stranger. The two friends who had seen her there had left before she did, so there was no assurance that she had gone with the stranger who bought her ale.

But he fit perfectly the description Wally had obtained from the Howard Johnson's staff: absolutely nondescript. He was white, they got that much, and somewhere between his early thirties and late forties, but beyond that he was only average to tall (difficult to judge slumped over a bar or a registration desk), dark to brown hair, normal complexion, normal weight, normal features.

Ten million people in New York City, excluding visitors from consideration for a moment. Five million are male, one third are white; that leaves two million. Limit the age to the thirties and forties, that comes to maybe half a million, give or take a hundred thousand. Dark hair—or maybe brown—and no distinguishing features (which eliminates the half dozen or so men scarred in hotel fires, and the few hundred scarred in knife fights), and we're down to maybe three hundred thousand.

Now add in the visitors. Back up to ten million.

So much for the statistical approach to criminal detection.

No one had seen Sally Forest leave Mcsorley's. Possibly she had left with the man who was buying her ale. No one had seen her again until she arrived at the Howard Johnson's. It didn't signify, however, that the man in Mcsorley's had been the killer. Certainly at *some* time during that evening she had been picked up by a man who had taken her to the hotel, had taken her to bed, had spent a reasonably calm evening with her—no torn bedclothes or clothing, no shattered furniture, no obscene lipstick messages scrawled on the mirror. The man had then, while she was asleep, strangled her.

What kind of a maniac does a thing like that? For no reason.

For no reason? Yes, Wally was reasonably sure of that. He had spent the last two days becoming an expert on Ms. Forest, and there was nothing in her life to lead to this end. He wouldn't have been surprised if she had been murdered in a fit of jealous rage, but the evidence in the hotel room did not fit such a scenario.

She had gone to bed with her murderer and she had made love to him (evidence obtained via vaginal exam), and she had been strangled without much of a struggle, taken completely by surprise, probably asleep when the fingers circled her throat, right thumb on the right carotid artery. She was unconscious within thirty seconds and dead within no more than two minutes after that. The bedclothes had hardly been rumpled, the blanket pulled neatly up and arranged under her chin.

Who had done it? Jack the Ripper, punishing her because she was sexually sinful? No, because the killer had first made love to her. A middle-class Westchester businessman who had been carrying on an affair with her and whose wife she was now threatening to call? No, he hadn't found anyone like that in her background, and it didn't fit anything he had learned of her character. So who?

Who was left? Dr. Jekyll and Mr. Hyde? A normal, respectable citizen out for an evening of pleasure and sin, transforming spontaneously into a murderous personality?

He got up and walked over to the window. He looked out. The view from here showed a normal, prosaic, dull little world.

He liked this view.

Dr. Jekyll and Mr. Hyde?

Oh, Christ.

Oh thank you, Christ Jesus, for this and all our blessings.

PART TWO

CHARLES LAUGHTON

CHAPTER

1

It was early December, and the weather was lovely. Old-time weather, the kind you don't get anymore. Cold but crisp, not a cloud in the sky, and the sky itself visible and bright blue. Peter and Katie walked through the park all the way to the Frick, then walked again down Fifth and had hot chocolate at the Stage Deli, and the day was so gorgeous they didn't even bitch about the overpricing.

She had taken a vacation day, in order to watch the program this morning, but he still had to work. And so at four o'clock Katie went shopping and he left for the Café du Mille.

Peter finished there about midnight, and went home to his own pad. He thought about calling her, just to talk about the lovely day they had had together, but it was late and she was probably asleep. He undressed and went to bed.

He got into bed, lay on his back, closed his eyes, and was asleep in two minutes.

And awake in half an hour.

His eyes opened, and he lay there and looked around the room.

He listened, but heard nothing; he had not been awakened by the subliminal sound of an intruder. The night air was cool but not cold, the window was open just a fraction. The sounds outside were, if anything, reassuring rather than disturbing.

Nothing was wrong. He turned over on his side and closed his eyes.

Five minutes later he turned onto his other side.

Then he tried lying on his belly.

He curled into the fetal position.

He stretched out on his back again.

Shit. It was going to be one of those nights.

He tried to clear his mind, think of nothing, but that didn't work. So he focused on what was wrong. Something must be bothering him. He tried to think what it could be.

Something was there, he knew it. But he couldn't locate it.

At about two o'clock his stomach began to hurt. Then the skin on his legs began to crawl, and by four o'clock in the morning he was suffering a full-fledged anxiety attack. He lay frightened and alone in his bed, helpless before the fury of his fear. Helpless not only because he was alone, but because he could not understand what was happening. Because, strictly speaking, it was not he who was afraid but the thing inside.

She was on the trail of a murderer who had struck in several cities. How long would it take her to realize that the murder in Milwaukee five years ago had occurred while he was there playing in *Salesman*? The murder in Louisville three years ago had occurred while he was stage managing there. The murder on the Cape . . .

The beast inside saw the threat clearly, and the same thought that spied the threat formulated the solution. The threat must be extinguished.

But Peter, lying awake in his bed, tossing with the anxieties that rocked him, could not face that thought. He could not let it surface. His mind refused to acknowledge it. And so his mind sought desperately another reason for his anxiety.

It kept close to the cause, but could not fasten directly on it. All he allowed himself to know was that he was afraid, that he was in danger, and somehow it was Katie's fault.

But how could it be Katie's fault? How could he possibly be anxious about Katie? Katie loved him—

Did Katie love him?

Idiot. How could she love him if she was planning to leave him?

And she *was* leaving him. He saw that now with a terrible clarity imparted by the lonely night. She was no longer an actress, she had told him as much.

"I used to be an actress. Now I'm a librarian."

"No! You still go out on auditions—"

"That was six months ago and I didn't get the job and I didn't even want *the job—"*

She didn't even want the job.

She is a librarian. She is leaving him, leaving the profession, she is going to be a real librarian and marry a schoolteacher from Schenectady and wear glasses . . . . She is leaving him.

She doesn't love him. She doesn't want to be tied to an itinerant out-of-work actor.

She doesn't love me anymore.

He slipped into sleep, slipped out of it again. He tossed and turned and no longer knew whether he was awake or asleep, thinking or dreaming. He knew that he was afraid, that something terrible was happening. He did not know that the beast inside was thrusting up, he did not know that he was struggling to keep it down. To acknowledge the existence of the beast was to surrender to it. He knew without admitting it that Katie was his only hope. The firmness of his grasp on sanity depended on her. She was his link to the real world. He couldn't let her go. He mustn't let her go.

If she leaves him he will be helpless against the beast, he knows this.

And, below, the beast knows it too.

In the morning it was all different. He woke slowly, gave a convulsive shudder, then lay quietly in bed. He looked around at the same old reassuring furniture. Everything was as it always had been. There was no danger.

He took a deep breath and relaxed.

God, what a night! Nightmares, certainly. The details were lost. He remembered only the anxiety, the fear. And now he was awake again and it had been only a nightmare after all and the world was all right again.

He got out of bed and went to the kitchen, conscious with each step of the pleasure of a pain-free body, an unfettered soul. Everything worked, everything was all right. His toes worked, his fingers worked, his legs worked. Nightmares are no terror to grown men, only to children. Because the poor children have not yet developed a sense of the divisor between the worlds of reality and illusion. In children they are joined, and therefore desperately frightening.

How wonderful it is to have escaped from that terrible world of childhood.

He filled the coffeepot with water, carried it to the stove, placed it there—

It slipped. Fell from his fingers, knocked against his leg, and cracked open on the floor.

His fingers shook. They didn't work. The room began to spin in upon him. He threw his hands out to steady himself—

But they wouldn't move.

The water from the coffeepot was spreading over the floor and he couldn't stop it, the coffee was etching its way through the floor, the whole building would collapse and he was trapped.

He ran out of the kitchen, grabbed his ski jacket and woolen cap from the hall closet and ran out of the apartment, slamming the door behind him, not even checking to be sure the lock had caught. He couldn't wait for the elevator. He ran down the steps and out into the street.

Across the sidewalk to the curb. Stepped out into the street—a cab came roaring up into the intersection, racing through without slowing, horn bellowing. Peter jumped back, struck something, turned amid a deluge of packages. Stunned, frightened, he stood there while they fell all around him. Stood there while the fat woman looked at him, at her groceries spread on the sidewalk and dumped in the street, while she began to scream. A terrible din was reverberating off the buildings and the streets. But he couldn't hear anything.

A crowd was gathering. The fat woman lifted both

hands, fists clenched, screaming silently at him.

He ran across the street with a truck plunging down on him. Tripped on the curb on the other side, nearly fell, caught himself and ran down the block, away from the screaming fat lady, to the luncheonette in the next block. He ducked inside.

It was warm and steamy, the windows clouded with moisture. Everything was in order. The people were sitting in the few booths or at the counter, the waitresses were moving back and forth between them, the cook in the far corner was frying eggs and bacon. No one looked at him.

He stood inside the door, breathing deeply. Then he sat down at the counter and ordered eggs sunny-side up, home fries and bacon, and whole wheat toast and coffee. Lots and lots of hot coffee.

Katie loves him. He sees that clearly now, in the cozy warmth of the friendly luncheonette, where everything is as it always was.

Katie has always loved him. They go back a long way, he and Katie. Back to early days in this cold city, when all they had to keep body and soul together was a shared bowl of soup and a dream.

(Music, hearts and flowers, up and out.) Peter smiles.

They still share that dream, damn it, they do. They still belong to each other. She's playing the part of a librarian now, that's all. She could no more stop loving him than she could stop breathing.

He choked.

The coffee must have gone down the wrong way. A terrible thought had slipped up for a moment but was quickly stamped down again. He would not permit the beast to think that thought. Not Katie.

He was quite sure of her love. He did not have to test it. It *could* be tested, of course, nothing easier. But there was no need. No need at all. Though certainly if he wanted to, he was clever enough to do so without her discovering what he was up to. To test her love . . .

That was as close as he would come to thinking it out, to verbalizing his ensuing actions. He never really meant to do any of it.

And so he finished his coffee, smiled at the waitress, paid his bill, left a tip, and turned around and walked across the restaurant toward the door but stopped without thinking by the phone booth in the corner and pulled out a dime and dialed her number.

If he hadn't had the dime, if he had been forced to go back to the cashier and ask for change, if he had planned his actions in advance, it might never have happened.

But he had the dime.

In this way, convulsively, compulsively, such things begin.

Katie had slept late. The library was open till nine and she was on the last shift. At the time Peter was struggling out of his nightmare-filled sleep she was sitting up in bed with a cup of coffee and the morning paper, and the phone rang.

It was Madame Szilardi. She was in the neighborhood and wondered if Katie would join her for breakfast at Schrafft's. Katie was surprised but happy to hear from her; it was one of those mornings when everything is pleasant. "I tell you what," she said. "I went out yesterday afternoon to Zabar's, to celebrate the television show I suppose, and I bought all kinds of cheeses and breads and pâté and some gorgeous stuff I've never even heard of, and I've just now made a fresh pot of coffee. Come up here and we'll have a feast."

"Oh that's darling of you, dear. I'd love a feast. And a chat?"

"Yes, of course," Katie laughed. "We'll chat all you like."

Katie showered and dressed and was just laying the table when the doorbell rang. She opened it and Madame Szilardi burst in—the thought occurred to Katie that she couldn't visualize Madame Szilardi simply walking into a room, she would always burst in—and grabbed Katie with both her hands and looked deeply into her eyes. She stared for a few seconds, then stepped back and removed her hat and cloak. "I'm so glad to see you're all right," she said.

"You're looking rather chipper yourself," Katie replied, hanging up the lovely old-fashioned mackintosh. "What a lovely cloak."

"Pure wool. Warmest thing on earth, don't you see? Can't understand why some women want furs. Skins of dead animals." She shivered. "Revolting."

"Barbaric," Katie agreed. "A throwback."

"Exactly."

"Come in and have some coffee."

"Thank you, I shall." She hesitated for just a moment. "You did promise a feast?"

Katie laughed and led her into the parlor, where all of Zabar's goodies were stacked. Madame Szilardi's face brightened, and Katie realized that she had already begun to like this rather fey old lady.

They buttered their bialies and took tomatoes and several different cheeses, and Katie poured the coffee.

Madame Szilardi sighed and said, "This is absolutely delightful."

"I'm glad you dropped in, Madame Szilardi."

"Cynthia. Madame Szilardi is only my professional name."

"Oh, I didn't know. What's your real name?"

"No, you don't understand. My name is Cynthia Szilardi. I meant, I'm not a madame." She actually blushed. "I mean—"

"Yes, I do understand," Katie said.

"A professional *title*, is what I mean."

Katie smiled.

"That sort of thing impresses one's clients, don't you see?" Madame Szilardi pressed on, eager that there be no misunderstanding. "It doesn't mean anything."

They chatted on and gorged themselves while Peter was flying out of his apartment and down the street to the luncheonette. They ate and talked and became good friends and were just deciding to share at least one more Danish as Peter paid his bill and then walked across the restaurant toward the door, stopped by the phone booth, reached into his pocket and found a dime.

They were deciding between the cheese Danish and the blueberry as he dialed.

The phone rang.

Madame Szilardi jumped.

Katie had just taken a bite of the cheese Danish.

She chewed quickly and swallowed and started to get up.

Madame Szilardi grabbed her by the hand.

Katie looked at her quizzically.

Madame Szilardi looked embarrassed.

"Anything wrong?" Katie asked.

"Danger," she muttered.

"What?"

"I don't know! I'm frightened."

The phone was ringing.

"It's only the phone."

"Don't answer it!"

"It's only the phone," Katie said, gently disengaging her hand. "It can't hurt you."

"Yes, of course," she admitted reluctantly. "You must be right. I suppose I'm wrong. I'm so often wrong."

Katie got up and walked across the floor and Madame Szilardi looked desperately around the room, searching for some other sign. She was probably wrong, but she *was* terrified.

Katie picked up the receiver.

"Hello," she said.

At that second, when she answered the phone, without premeditation he slipped unconsciously into a perfect imitation of Charles Laughton. He would never know why. But the voice—soft, suave and yet rough and rasping, both polite and menacing—just seemed to fit the occasion.

"Katie?" he asked. "Katherine McGregor Townsend?"

"Yes," Katie said, swallowing the last of the Danish, smiling reassuringly at Madame Szilardi—*see, it's only the phone, it can't hurt us*—"yes, it's me."

"Ah, my name is Wilder," Peter said. "Charles Wilder. I'm a . . . sort of a friend of a friend, my dear."

Katie lifted her eyebrows and shrugged at Madame Szilardi and asked, "What friend of which friend?"

But he didn't want to make up a relationship with someone she might have known. Because the whole point was not to find out if she would be polite to an old friend of a friend, but to find out if she would be receptive to any new offers, if she could be picked up over the phone by any phony, if she loved him or if she was planning to leave him and therefore looking for a replacement. To find out if she was *available*.

And so he turned on the charm. It fit in perfectly with the timbre of the Charles Laughton voice, and he was totally in character from those first few words. He could do it easily enough, he could be charming when he wanted, he knew how to play these verbal games, and so instead of answering her question he led her in and out and up and down.

He tried to make the voice sound sexy. He tried to put intimations of immorality into innocent words, but he wasn't quite able to do Charles Laughton and sex at the same time. The charm oozed through, sufficiently imperative, and Katie talked to him.

They chatted.

Peter enjoyed the anonymity. The power inherent in the situation, knowing who she was while remaining, so to speak, invisible himself.

Katie would have ended the conversation at the beginning had it not been for Madame Szilardi, who sat there looking at her with frightened eyes. The sweet old lady might not have accurate powers of psychic telepathy, but she was a sensitive old thing and all her senses were extended toward Katie because of this silly fear. She would very likely sense that something was wrong if Katie cut off the call and hung up, and Katie didn't want to frighten her.

So she talked on for the first few minutes, and that was enough. Peter's charm—Charles Laughton's charm—began to take effect. Katie smiled, at first despite herself, and then willingly.

"I'm not really a friend of a friend," he admitted. "If I were I should simply ask for an introduction. I've only seen you at the library. I've sat and watched you there for hours."

"Why not just walk up and introduce yourself?"

"Oh, my dear, I couldn't." A voice so sad. "I could never do that. I'm much too shy."

Katie was kind to him. He sounded like an older man, cultured, lonely. Talking to him, looking with calm reassurance at Madame Szilardi, Katie was struck with the idea that it might be mutually beneficial to introduce the two of them.

She was smiling at the idea when he asked if she might one day condescend to meet him? Perhaps for lunch? Perhaps today?

She hadn't been picked up so casually in years. But there had been a time, in her actress days, when she met new people easily and often. Sometimes they became friends. Still, her first, instinctive reaction was to say no.

And yet, she thought, he's obviously *safe*. There was no danger in that soft cultured voice.

She looked at Madame Szilardi. What a coup it would be if she could bring two elderly, lonely people together.

She put her hand over the receiver and whispered, "Are you free today at three?"

Madame Szilardi, uncomprehending, nodded assent.

Katie said into the phone, "I'm working the late

shift today, so I can't break for lunch until three. Would that be all right?"

The voice said yes, that would be perfect.

And so they arranged to meet at Schrafft's on Fifth Avenue, near the library.

What could be more innocuous than that?

Bitch.

Bitch! he screamed silently at the telephone receiver now lying silent and disconnected in its cradle on the wall.

Bitch! he screamed silently at the uncomprehending universe, and walked out of the luncheonette onto the cold streets.

Three o'clock.

Peter was in his bedroom, sitting on the bed.

Katie was sitting alone in Schrafft's, waiting.

She *is* his Katie, isn't she?

Perhaps she was only fooling old Charles Laughton. Perhaps she only wanted to get rid of him, perhaps she never had any intention of meeting him, of keeping their assignation?

Perhaps.

He nodded. Tentatively at first, then emphatically.

Probably!

Definitely probably.

Peter got up and pulled on his jacket and left the apartment.

To see for himself.

Three-thirty.

Katie and Madame Szilardi were seated at their table in Schrafft's. They were sharing an open tuna sandwich with melted cheese, and a pot of tea with lemon. They were chatting away furiously, and had by now forgotten the man on the telephone, who was evidently too shy to show up for their meeting.

Katie felt a momentary pang of sadness for him, locked away in his lonely little world, and then she forgot him. He probably had made telephone dates like this before, with cashiers at the movies or waitresses or salesgirls, he talked to them on the phone but never had the courage to meet them. It was all very sad.

The world was full of sad and lonely people, but here in Schrafft's Madame Szilardi—Cynthia—was bright and talkative and amusing; it was warm and cozy and the tuna with melted cheese on crisp rye bread went perfectly with the tea, and it was really very pleasant.

By three-thirty she had forgotten about the lonely man on the tlephone.

Three-thirty.

Peter was standing outside Schrafft's, looking in through the plate-glass window.

With a sick shock in the pit of his stomach he saw Katie at her table in the corner, and she was with somebody else—

At first he thought the other person at the table was the man who called her on the phone: she had met him, they were talking and laughing together, laughing at him—

And then he realized that couldn't be, *he* was the man on the telephone.

It was cold standing there, but he began to sweat. He mustn't let the man on the phone become too real.

That sometimes happened with an actor, he knew; sometimes the character on stage acquires an independent reality in the actor's mind—

He shook himself.

Never mind. That was not important. What was important was not the illusion in his mind but the reality in Schrafft's. The reality in Schrafft's was Katie.

Katie sitting there, keeping her date, waiting for the telephone voice to materialize and sit down beside her.

Bitch, he whispered.

Oh, bitch, he whispered over and over as he walked down Forty-sixth Street to his job at the Café du Mille.

Midnight.

The witching hour.

Peter returned to his apartment, walked straight through to the bedroom, sat down heavily on the bed. His job as a waiter was a physical one, and he was exhausted. But the prospect of sleep did not attract him. Instead, the night stretched ahead of him, bleakly empty.

He was angry, and he was afraid.

The night stretched to a black infinity before him, empty without Katie. It was all her fault, after all.

He reached toward the night table, picked up the telephone.

Katie was asleep when it rang. Her eyes blinked open, but it took two or three more rings before she was awake enough to identify the sound.

"Hello," she mumbled.

"Ah, I'm sorry, dear," Charles Laughton said.

"Didn't mean to wake you. Do you know who this is?"

"No, who is it? What time is it?"

"Are you sleepy, love? Terribly sorry. Are you in bed?"

"Of course I'm in bed!" She was awake now, and angry. "Who is it?"

"Don't you really know?"

The voice was familiar. Oh God, yes, she remembered now. Her lonely old man. Damn, was he going to become a nuisance?

"Is that you?" She couldn't think of his name.

"Yes, it's me, Charles. You were a naughty girl this afternoon."

"What are you talking about?"

"We had a date. You stood me up."

"I did not. I was there."

"Oh, well, yes, you were there. But not alone."

"What difference did that make? I was with a friend."

"Why? Were you afraid to meet me alone?"

"Of course not. Why should I be afraid?"

"Why, indeed?"

"Were you there?"

"Obviously. Since I saw you with your friend."

"Why didn't you come over to our table?"

Pause.

"Look, Charles," she said, "it's really late and I was asleep, I think maybe we'd better just forget the whole thing. Good night."

"Meet me tomorrow? For lunch?"

Pause.

"No," she said. "I don't think so."

"Schrafft's," he said.

"No. There's no point—"

"I'll be waiting for you."

"Charles—"

"What?"

She hesitated. She didn't know what he looked like, but she thought she could visualize him. She sighed. Hell. When she was a kid she always got into trouble by bringing home stray animals, homeless animals. But she wasn't a kid any longer.

"I'm not sure I can make it," she said.

"I'll wait for you," he said.

She capitulated, without acknowledging it. "How will I know who you are?" she asked.

"Oh, you'll recognize me all right," he said. "I'll be the one who looks like he wants to fuck you."

And he hung up.

Peter woke in the morning fully clothed. After the phone call he had simply stretched out on the bed and fallen asleep. He sat up and picked up the telephone all in one movement.

He glanced at the clock. It was nearly eight. She'd be leaving soon for work. He had to find whether she would run out to meet any son of a bitch who just called up out of nowhere to tell her he wants to fuck her.

She picked up the phone on the third ring.

"Hi," he said. "It's me."

"Hi yourself," she said, cheerfully. "What's new in the world of French cuisine?"

"*Im Westen nichts neues.* You sound peppy this morning."

"Why not? I'm treating myself to a whole English muffin and an egg and cheese."

"You'll get fat."

"I *am* fat."

"You're gorgeous."

"*That's* why I'm happy. Because strange men call me first thing in the morning to tell me I'm gorgeous."

"Strange men call you?"

There. That led into it innocently enough. Now she had her chance to tell him all about it, to tell him about the strange man who is bothering her, to ask for his protection.

"*You're* the strange man," she said. "You're a very strange man."

So.

He waited.

She said nothing else.

"Well," he said, "I just called to see how you were."

"Thank you kindly," she said. "I'm just fine. When shall we get together?"

"I don't know." He paused a moment, then blurted out, "I saw you yesterday."

"Where?"

"In Schrafft's."

"Were you there?"

"No, I was just passing by. I saw you through the window."

"Why didn't you come in?"

"I was late for work. Besides, you were with somebody."

"Oh, that was Madame Szilardi! You would love her. I wish you had come in."

"How about meeting me for lunch today?"

She hesitated for just a second, then said, "Sure. Fine. I'll see if she can join us, in fact. I know you'll love her."

So it was all right, then. She had no intention of meeting the voice.

"Great," he said. "Where shall we eat?"

This time she hesitated a bit longer. And then she said, "How about Schrafft's?"

Oh, bitch, he thought.

"Is that all right?" she asked.

"Yes," he said. "Why not?"

"You sound funny."

"No. I'm just smiling."

"Why are you smiling?"

"I don't know. I just think you're cute."

There.

She felt better now. Thank God for Peter.

She had actually been frightened when the telephone rang. She had been sure it would be Charles. What would she say to him?

With that one penultimate word of their last conversation everything had changed.

She laughed, and then laughed at herself for laughing. Yes, now that she felt safe again it was easy to laugh. Still it *was* funny, in a way. That a man saying *fuck* to her should frighten her. The word was standard in the lexicon of her quondam profession, she could think of several directors who couldn't enunciate the simplest stage movement without using it twice.

But it was the context. It had changed everything.

With that one word the entire character of her phantom caller had altered. Everything about him that had evoked pity before now evoked . . . not terror, that was much too strong a word, but perhaps *queasiness*.

He now seemed an old, lonely, shy, *sick* man.

But it was all right. Peter would be with her now. She didn't want simply not to show up for their appointment. What good would that do? He would just call her again. She had to find out who he was. What he looked like.

So she would go to Schrafft's with Peter, and with Madame Szilardi too, if she was free. And even if Charles was frightened off again, she'd spot him this time. She'd keep her eyes open. She was sure she'd be able to pick him out in the crowd of bourgeois middle-aged ladies who formed the Schrafft's clientele.

He'd surely be easy to recognize, even if he didn't approach her. She remembered what he said. He'd be the one who looked like—

She shivered.

CHAPTER

2

Wally Gilford thought about time.

He walked down Fifth Avenue. Today was his birthday. What else are you going to think about when you're forty-seven years old and your wife has been dead for ten years and your daughter is somewhere up in Massachusetts? And it's early December and they're putting up the Christmas decorations on Fifth Avenue.

He smiled. Several pedestrians pushing past him on the crowded street glanced at him and moved quickly away. Smiling people on the streets of New York are probably dangerous.

But Wally was smiling because the Christmas decorations reminded him of his wife's telling him during the spring that if he didn't pull down the Christmas decorations and put the Christmas tree away soon, they'd be putting up the decorations on Fifth Avenue again before he took his down.

Time is a funny thing. There was an article in the *Times* just last Sunday, about whether or not time really exists.

Matter is made up of particles called atoms, and energy is made up of particles called quanta, and the question is, if time really exists, shouldn't it also be made of particles? They call these particles chronons, but nobody knows if they exist. No one has ever been able to find one.

If the chronons don't exist, does time exist? If time doesn't exist, what is it that separates him from his wife, Wally wonders. If time doesn't exist, it must be only his imagination that separates them. But no, that can't be right. Wally shakes his head and again the people on the sidewalk near him glance at him and edge away as they hurry along. No that can't be right, Wally thinks, because it's his imagination that connects him to her.

At first he thought he'd never forget her. Everyone said he was looking at it the wrong way. He might never forget her, but he would forget the pain, the loss. He'd learn to live without her, he'd learn to live again. He was young, they all said. He'd find another woman in time.

But time is a funny thing, whether it exists or not, and they were wrong. He *did* forget her. He forgot what she looked like. When he thought of her sometimes in the middle of the night, he couldn't picture her face exactly, her expression. He had to get out of bed and turn on the light and look at the pictures.

What he didn't forget was the pain, the loss.

Another funny thing was that the time that governed his daughter's growing somehow got out of sync with the time that governed the fading of his wife, because they never quite crossed each other. His daughter had grown up into a young lady before he had the time to look and lust after other young ladies, and now it was too late.

He couldn't see himself settling down with any of the middle-aged matrons that time told him were his own age. And he couldn't go chasing after youngsters his daughter's age. Sweet innocent young girls who got themselves strangled in hotel rooms.

He had filed the folder away this morning. Nothing new had happened in the last couple of days. Whether or not time existed, it was on the side of the murderers. Time silently rolled on and covered up the trail of the killer.

What was he going to buy his daughter for Christmas? She insisted she didn't need a car at the University of Massachusetts, but he couldn't imagine living in the wilds of Amherst without the independence a car gave you. It wasn't like New York, after all.

If he was a lieutenant he could buy her a car. But he had been a plain old detective sergeant for twenty years now, now and forever. He was the smartest detective on the force, he could pass the lieutenant's exam in his sleep, and if you passed the exam promotion was automatic. But he had never signed up to take the exam. He never would.

He was crossing Forty-eighth Street and he turned sharply to his right before he realized why, before his mind caught up to his legs, which had followed his glancing eyes without hesitation. He realized then that that bit of white and blue parked down the block was a 1966 Chevy. You didn't hardly see a car like that anymore, but its shape was etched firmly in his mind. It triggered a spasm of response every time his eyes picked it up.

His wife had been killed by a 1966 Chevy. Not a

white and blue one, but it wasn't going to be the same color after all these years. It would have been painted many times, many colors. If it still existed.

It had existed once, long enough to roar away from the curb and across the street and onto the sidewalk and strike his wife as she stood there staring in paralyzed fear. She had only been passing by. She had been walking down a typical New York street on a typical New York spring night, passing a typical New York liquor store which was at that precise moment being subjected to a typical New York robbery. She had stopped and stared through the lit plate-glass windows at the sight of the clerk with his hands in the air, and a moment later she was staring at the sight of the clerk with the back of his head blown away, splattering blood and brains and hair and skin over the bottles on the wall behind him. She was still standing there staring as the man (men? no witnesses left alive to tell) came running out of the store and into the Chevy; she was standing there as the man or men must have seen her and as they/he roared away from the curb, and swerved the Chevy across the street and onto the sidewalk and into and over her, knocking her sprawling into the gutter, splattering her head as it hit the curbstone.

A witness down the street had heard the Chevy screech, had seen it careen down the dark street. It had left Peggy broken in the gutter and had roared off into the night and had disappeared into the years.

He still stopped every time he saw a '66 Chevy. He still walked down the block and squatted by the side of it and peered under its right front fender to look for signs of an accident, of body work. He knew what to look for. He had gone over it with the auto lab people in the department, the people who had told him long ago to forget it, there was no way the car was going to still exist, it was rusting away on a junk pile somewhere in Arizona or Wyoming or wherever.

He believed them. He knew he'd never find that Chevy. But he still walked down the block and squatted and looked under the right front fender of every '66 Chevy he came across. Not with any hope. It was just a ritual he went through, the way he knelt down for a moment every time he entered St. Patrick's to get out of the cold on an early winter morning.

He walked back to Fifth Avenue and continued his way downtown. The girl was dead and her case was dead, her folder was filed away, and there was other work to do. He was headed toward Thirty-seventh Street to check an electronic store break-in. That was the beauty of being a cop in New York City these days, there was never a lack of something to occupy your time.

He passed Schrafft's, he glanced inside. It was lunch time and he had skipped breakfast. He glanced at the menu in the window. He grimaced. He wasn't that hungry.

He'd walk two more blocks and get some fried smelts at Paddy's.

CHAPTER

3

Inside Schrafft's it was warm and cozy. Madame Szilardi had arrived first and taken the same table Katie and she had occupied yesterday. She considered that a good omen.

She nodded meaningfully to herself. Good omens were not that easy to come by. This case had been characterized by bad omens right from the beginning, right from the time of the television broadcast when she had become so frightened . . . She clucked at herself. She was referring to *this case* already, when it was nothing of the sort. It was just a fright, a worry, a bad dream.

She took a deep breath and pushed the thoughts away. The table, at any rate, was a good omen. Sufficient unto the day, she thought, and nodded vigorously to herself and ordered an Amaretto sour and settled back to read the menu and wait for little Katie.

It was an interesting menu, but of course the prices were shocking. Some people, she knew, ate at Schrafft's frequently, several times a year. She couldn't understand the indulgence.

She chided herself for that. The sin of arrogance. And not to forget, today was the second day she was indulging herself at the very same table. They'd soon be naming it after her.

Well no, that wasn't quite fair, really it wasn't. She could hardly be said to be indulging herself. She was here only to warn Katie. There were things Katie had to be told.

Katie was in danger, that had to be said. No mincing of words there, straight to the point.

She sighed.

The trouble was, a statement like that led naturally to several queries. What danger? How do you know?

Oh dear.

How to explain?

Katie was a darling, and a polite little thing, but it was clear she didn't understand the metaphysical dimensions of existence. Her interpretation of dreams would be merely Freudian.

Madame Szilardi went over in her own mind the dream she had had last night, looking at it from a Freudian point of view.

She nearly blushed.

A huge bird swooping down on her, with a stiff beak—well, she had read Freud. She knew what *that* would symbolize. She looked quickly around the restaurant, hoping nobody could read her mind.

But never mind; all that's neither here nor there, she told herself. The important aspect of the dream was the sense of pervasive danger. If only she could remember that part more clearly. She had been holding something in her hand . . . a telephone! She had been clutching a hard, shiny telephone in her hand.

She shook her head sadly. She knew how *that* symbolism would be interpreted.

Back to square one. This was exactly the position she had been in this morning, wondering how to tell Katie, when the phone had rung and Katie had asked her to lunch to meet a friend of hers, the young man Peter.

Perhaps he would believe. Perhaps he'd be able to help.

When Peter arrived at the restaurant he found Katie so deep in conversation with this other woman that she didn't even notice he was standing beside them. Funny Katie. She comes to a restaurant to find a man who wants to fuck her, and then she sits talking her head off to an old woman and not even noticing when someone comes up and stands right next to her. Funny Katie, Peter thought, silly bitch. He could be anyone at all, standing there. He could have a knife in his hand, he could—

He bent over and kissed her, lightly on the cheek.

She jumped, and then smiled up at him. "Oh, Peter, we were just talking about you. Cynthia," she said to the older woman, "this is my friend Peter. Peter, this is Madame Szi—"

Madame Szilardi jumped from her seat and stood for a moment staring at Peter. Her eyes were wide, her voice whispering but urgent. "There is danger," she whispered hoarsely. "There is much danger hovering over our Katie."

She came around the side of the table, grasped his hand fervently, and looked deeply into his eyes. Then she closed her eyes, the better to feel his vibrations.

She held on to his hand with both of her own, eyes closed, as Peter looked over her white head at Katie, who smiled and shook her head in warning, shrugged her shoulders helplessly, finally nearly laughed.

"There is great danger," Madame Szilardi announced, then opened her eyes, stared unblinkingly one more moment at Peter's face, and suddenly relaxed. "But not from you. No." She turned and confidently assured Katie, still holding on to Peter's hand. "No, this young man is not dangerous."

"I never for a moment thought he was," Katie said.

"Can never be sure," Madame Szilardi said. "Better safe than sorry." She patted Peter's hand and relinquished it, sitting down again at the table. "Won't you join us?" she asked.

"Thank you, I will. Tell me, how do you *know* I'm not dangerous?"

"Vibrations," Madame Szilardi said, and buttered her roll.

"Cynthia is a psychic," Katie began.

"Medium," Madame Szilardi corrected her.

"Oh," Peter said. "Is that how you know there is a danger hovering over Katie?"

Madame Szilardi nodded, her mouth full of buttered roll. She chewed and swallowed. "I really shouldn't eat this," she said. "I had a dream, you see."

"About buttered rolls?"

"Peter," Katie warned.

"The buttered rolls have nothing to do with it. I dreamed about Katie."

"I often dream about Katie."

"But you," Madame Szilardi pointed out, "are not a medium."

Peter seemed slightly hurt. "How do you know I'm not?"

"It's all there in the vibrations. Now back to my dream—"

"Your dream told you there is a danger surrounding our Katie? What kind of danger?"

Madame Szilardi looked somewhat abashed. "I'm not exactly sure," she admitted. "Understanding the meaning of dreams is more of an art than a science, you know. But quite distinctly there was a pervading sense of danger." She leaned across the table and whispered the word again for emphasis. *"Danger."*

Peter smiled and shook his head. "There can't be any danger for Katie. Everybody loves Katie. Even strangers love Katie."

"Strangers?" He was gratified that Katie picked up on the word immediately. "What strangers?" she asked.

"Don't be modest, love. It's your smile. Or maybe your eyes. Or maybe it's your eyes *and* your smile. The effect is immediate and overwhelming. Everybody loves you. I'll bet there's not a man in this restaurant who doesn't love you."

He half stood and craned his neck around. There was one man seated by himself on the other side of the room. "I'll bet if you just walked by that man's table," he said, "I'll bet he'd be in love with you."

Madame Szilardi laughed. Katie said, "Don't be silly, Peter. Madame Szilardi doesn't know when you're joking."

"Cynthia," Madame Szilardi said. "You really must call me Cynthia."

Peter smiled. His eyes hadn't left Katie's face, and he had seen her look across the room at the man and then look quickly away again. *Is that him?* she was wondering. Her behavior was so terrible it was delicious. All through the meal that followed, all through the bantering conversation—for Madame Szilardi had given up trying to convince them that there was *danger*—Katie smiled and talked and listened . . . and if he hadn't known, he would never have noticed her eyes blinking around the restaurant.

Blinking here, blinking there. Just a flicker of the eyes as her teeth bit into the hot pastrami and turkey club sandwich. Just the merest flicker of the eyes, every once in a while.

Looking for someone.

Peter had to smile.

She would never find him.

He called her again that evening.

"Hello, my dear," he said in his Charles Laughton voice. "Do you know who this is?"

"I'm sorry, I must have dozed off—"

Oh, the little dear! The sleep in her voice conjured up such tenderness, such innocence.

He sighed. False, all false.

"This is Charles," he said. "Remember? Lunch at Schrafft's?"

"Were you there?"

Ah, she was awake now!

"Yes, I was there. I am *always* there."

"I don't believe you."

"Don't you? Shall I describe your dress? Or shall I perhaps describe the sweet old lady and the effete gentleman whose company you so obviously preferred to my own?"

"I didn't see you—"

"Yes you did."

"I did not!"

"Oh my love, indeed you did. What you mean is, you didn't *recognize* me. You couldn't help but see me, the way you were continually looking around the restaurant. What is more difficult to understand is why you didn't recognize me. I am, you remember, the one who looks like he wants to fuck you."

"I'm not going to listen—"

"But perhaps it's not so difficult to understand after all. Perhaps everyone wants to fuck you. In that case you'll never recognize me, will you? You'll never know who I am. I could be anyone at all. I could be the man next to you in an elevator, or on the bus. I could be walking beside you as you enter the library, I could be one of the multitudinous whores sitting at the tables in the reading room, staring at you—oh my. Oh my, oh my. Did I say whores? Multitudinous whores? How silly. I meant to say *hordes*, of course, multitudinous hordes. Freudian slip. Why should I think of whores when I speak to you, do you think?"

"Don't talk like that."

"Do I shock you?"

"Is that what you're trying to do?"

"I don't think I could."

"No, you can't," she agreed. "Because I think I understand."

Understand? She *thinks* she understands? How can she understand him when she doesn't even know who he is?

He is suddenly terribly angry, and in the instant of its creation his anger bursts open and floods him with . . . pleasure? Yes, even in that moment of fury he is aware of the pleasure. He understands now. He is angry because he *can* be angry. He can be as furious as he wants, and there is nothing she can do about it. *She doesn't know who he is.* He can do anything, say anything. He is all-powerful.

"You understand nothing," he tells her quietly.

"You don't know me and you don't understand me. But I understand you, and I know you. Do you know what I see when I look at you? I see you naked—"

"I'm not going to listen to you talk like that—"

"In the restaurant I saw you naked. Right now I see you naked—"

She hung up.

The phone clicked in his ear.

He sat there holding it, breathing hard, trying to recover from the sudden anger.

He put the phone down. Went into the bathroom, washed his face with cold water.

That was better.

To prove his patience, to prove his control to himself, he sat on his bed and didn't touch the phone for five minutes.

Then he picked it up again.

Dialed her number.

It rang. It rang again and again.

Finally she picked it up. "Hello?"

"And do you know," he asked, as if they had never been disconnected, "what I'm going to do to you?"

He waited.

She didn't answer.

He hung up.

Sunday morning.

Early. Eight-fifteen. But he is awake.

In bed, but not alone.

He is aware of the heavy lump in bed with him.

Oh, God, he thinks. Who is it?

A sudden stab of terror. He can't remember—

She moves.

She stretches, turns over, looks at him.

It's all right. He remembers now.

Last night, at work till midnight. Then a quick drink at one place, another quick drink at another. At one of them he meets her. This girl. Name unknown, unremembered, unimportant. They are all the same.

She looks at him now. Smiles.

He turns away, sits up, gets out of bed.

"What are you doing?" Disappointed.

Christ.

"Thought I'd run out and get us some lox and bagels," he says.

"Lovely. If you go to Zabar's, get me a bialy."

He gets the lox and bagels, forgets the bialy, turns around and walks back two blocks to get it, passing two phone booths on the way.

There is a third phone booth before he reaches Zabar's.

He stops in front of it.

It's probably broken, anyway.

He shifts the bundle to his left hand, picks up the receiver, hears a dial tone. It isn't broken. Fate.

He drops in a dime, dials her number.

"Hello," Katie says.

"Did I wake you?"

"Yes. Who is this?"

He doesn't answer.

"Is that you?"

He doesn't answer. He begins to breathe loudly into the telephone. Louder and louder, faster and faster, going up to a climax. Then a soft groan, a sigh, and silence.

He hangs up.

He goes back to the apartment. The girl is up and dressed and has put on the coffee. She takes the bag he hands her and spreads the food out on the kitchen table.

"You forgot the bialy," she says.

Tuesday night, late. Wednesday morning, really, by the clock.

Peter had gone home after work, but couldn't sleep. His thoughts are with Katie. He walks the streets, down as far as Twenty-eighth, up to Central Park, west to Tenth Avenue, east all the way to the river. It is cold and the wind is biting, why the hell is he out here instead of sleeping quietly in his bed?

He dials her number.

The phone rings.

He can see it ringing. He can see it on the bed table, he can see Katie tucked deeply under the covers, startled by the ring, reaching out without thinking, reflex action, not yet awake, reaching out, fumbling, dark in the room, searching for the phone—

"Hello?"

And here he is, invader of the night, he is with her now. Too late, she recognizes the voice. Too late, she thinks she should have let it ring.

And so he is with her now, voice low, quietly authoritative, calm and invulnerable, invincible, a voice from the ages, with just a slight accent, barely a touch of a lisp, vaguely familiar—but from where? Can she recognize it?

Never. How could she associate it with old movies on the television?

A voice from the depths.

"Take off your clothes."

"Go away! Please go away."

"Take off your pajamas. I like to look at your body. But never mind, I can see your body all the time, can't I? I saw it yesterday."

"You didn't see me yesterday!"

"How do you know? You don't know who I am, do you? But I am always there. I was outside your building yesterday, as you came out. I am with you always—"

"Leave me alone!"

And she hangs up.

But he has another dime.

He dials her number again.

It rings. It rings and rings.

She does not answer.

He sees her cowering under the quilt, head buried, trying not to hear it ringing.

He lays the receiver down on the shelf and leaves the phone booth. Nobody at this time of night is likely to want this phone, it will ring until she gives up and answers it.

How long can she hold out? How long can she lie there alone in her apartment with the pillow pulled tightly around her ears, listening to it ring, knowing that he is at the other end waiting for her?

Finally, she will answer it.

And when she does, there will be no one there.

PART THREE

THE
DETECTIVE

CHAPTER

1

The next morning, when Katie called Peter and asked him to meet her for lunch at a restaurant on Forty-second Street, he burst out laughing. Half a century ago, Forty-second Street was the center of show business in this country—*Tell all the gang on Forty-second Street that I will soon be there*—but today it is only Deviate Street, Porno Street, Sick Street. So she explained that she meant Forty-second Street west of Tenth Avenue, and Forty-second west of Tenth is a different universe from Forty-second east of Eighth.

They met at La Rousse, next to the Director's Theater. Small, narrow, deep and dark, with a brick interior wall and clean tablecloths, and the best fish soup in the city.

"The soup is great," he agreed. "How are you?"

She smiled and nodded. "How about you?"

"Same old story," he said. "Always something new.

Always something in the wings. I'm up for a role at the East Side, it's an original play, melodrama type, not very good. But Pirie McDonald's directing, and I think I can make something of the role. If I get the part."

He lifted the tablecloth to make sure that the table was wood, and knocked on it twice. Katie tried to smile. These showcase productions do not pay the actors any salary, but they get a chance to exhibit their talents if they can con any agents or producers or casting directors uptown to watch the performance. "Will they let you take the time off from the restaurant?" she asked.

He shook his head. "I'll quit." He waited for her to tell him that he'd be quitting a good-paying, practically tax-free job for a harder job that paid nothing, but instead she just sat there, biting her lip.

"And how are things with you?" he asked.

"Oh, you know," she said. "Just like with you. Same old story, always something new."

"So what's new?"

She smiled and took a crust of the French bread, broke it off, chewed it. She said, "I've been getting obscene phone calls."

He looked at her. She looked out the window, at the people passing by on the sidewalk.

Poor thing, he thought. She's ashamed.

"Tell me," he said.

She reached across to the bread basket and broke off another chunk. She sat there breaking small pieces off, nibbling on them. After a while she said, "This man keeps calling me up."

"What man?"

"I don't know. He says his name is Charles something, but I never met him."

"What does he say?"

"Sometimes he doesn't say anything, he just breathes."

"Well, we all do that, you know."

"I mean he makes a sound like he's having an orgasm. It's frightening."

"Are you frightened?"

She nibbled at the bread crusts. "Yes," she said.

"But he doesn't say anything?"

She spread the broken pieces of crust on the white tablecloth. "Sometimes he does."

"What does he say?"

She arranged them in little piles. She picked at the piles. "He says he wants to fuck me."

"Just like that?"

"Yes, that's the whole point. That's why he calls me."

"But that's nothing to be upset about, love. Everyone wants to fuck you."

She smiled tightly. "That's all very well, but they shouldn't say so."

He laughed. "My, aren't we prim today?"

She laughed with him, and then suddenly she stopped. "But Peter, it's really not funny. It frightens me."

"Why don't you just hang up?"

"That's easy to say!"

"It's easy to do."

She looked down again at the bread crumbs. "Sometimes I hang up. It's hard to explain. It's hard to just hang up on him. You don't understand."

"Why is it hard?"

She didn't answer. She moved all the little crumbs from one pile to the other, then she reached over and took out another chunk of bread and broke off another piece of crust and began another little pile.

"Remember last week?" she asked. "We had lunch at Schrafft's? With Madame Szilardi?"

He nodded.

"He was there."

"Why didn't you point him out?"

"I don't know who he is! I don't know what he looks like!"

"Then how do you know he was there?"

"He had called me that morning. That's when it was all just starting, he wasn't being obscene then. I had sort of made a date to meet him there."

"No, your date was with me."

"That was after. He had called me first, that morning, to ask me to meet him for lunch there, and he wasn't obscene but he sounded kind of peculiar, you know? So after I had agreed and we hung up, I thought about it and decided I wasn't going to go. And then you called and asked me out for lunch and I thought if we went together I could see what he looked like."

"But we didn't meet anyone there. Except your friend Madame Szilardi."

"I know. He didn't show up. I mean, I don't know what he looks like and he didn't come over to us or say anything, but then later he called me up and said he had been there. He keeps calling me, nearly every day now, and says that he wants to fuck me and things like he's watching me or he can see me, he knows what I'm doing. I don't like it. I'm frightened."

"Do you want to call the police?"

"Do you think I should?"

He shrugged. "I don't know."

"It's so hard to talk about. It makes me feel dirty. It was hard even to tell you. I'd hate to have to talk to some policeman about it. What could they do, anyway?".

Peter looked at her.

"Maybe he'll just stop," she said.

"Yes," Peter said. "Maybe he'll just stop."

Ring.

She stares at the phone.

I am not afraid, she tells herself.

It's probably someone else, she says.

Suddenly she is angry. "I will *not* be a prisoner in my own apartment!" she says out loud.

She picks up the phone.

"The phone has been answered! Hello! Are you there? Hello!"

"Hello," she says.

"Am I speaking to Miss Katherine McGregor Townsend of Manhattan?"

"Yes. Who is this?"

"Miss Townsend, this is your lucky day, this is your lucky hour, and this is your lucky minute! Are you listening to radio station WQCR?"

"No."

"Well, that *is* unfortunate, but never mind! Just for having the good fortune to pick up your phone, you are being given the golden opportunity to win a consolation prize by answering a simple question! Are you ready?"

"Yes."

"All right then, here we go! Today's consolation prize is worth five hundred and thirty-five dollars in silver nickels, and it's all yours if you can tell me the final title the Earl of Leicester received from Queen Elizabeth while he was in the Tower awaiting execution! Can you tell me that?"

Silence.

"We're all waiting, Miss Townsend, America's radio audience is waiting for you to tell us the correct answer and collect five hundred and thirty-five dollars in silver nickels!"

"I'm sorry, I don't know the answer."

"Oh dear! Oh, that's really too bad, you dear little cocksucker."

She nearly screams.

Instead, she bangs down the phone.

"It's for you."

Two days later.

Three-thirty P.M.

The third floor of the New York Public Library, the main reading room. Katie is on desk duty, supervising a staff of four, mostly part-time student help. One of the students, a tall, husky, black boy named Kenneth, has answered the phone and is now holding it out to Katie. "It's for you," he says again.

She hesitates.

Kenneth smiles. "It's for *you*," he says.

"What did he say?" she asks.

"Who?"

She gestures toward the phone in his hand. "The man on the phone. Who did he ask for?"

"You."

"What did he *say*? Did he ask for me by name?"

"Right. Miss Townsend, he said, is she there?"

She takes the phone. "Hello?"

"Hello, my dear."

She feels a weakness in her legs. It is him. She looks around the room, she sees Kenneth looking at her. She doesn't want to make a scene. She says quietly, "I'm not allowed to receive personal calls here."

"Of course not. I'm sorry. But actually that's why I'm calling, to apologize. That wasn't a nice joke, was it?"

"What?"

"About the radio prize. I'm sorry. I don't know what gets into me."

"How did you know I'm here now?"

He chuckles. "That's my little secret. Shall I tell you?"

Silence.

"Shall I?"

"Yes."

"Ask me then. Politely."

"How did you know where I am?"

"Please?"

"Please."

"It's simple. I'm here, too."

She glances up, but that's silly. There are no public phones in the reading room. She looks around at the other staff members. None of them are using their phones.

"You're lying," she says.

Again that soft chuckle. "Actually I'm down the hall, in the phone booth at the end of the corridor."

She holds her breath, bites her lip.

Kenneth is standing by the file catalog, checking a reference for a reader. If only he'll look up—

Damn it, he won't!

"What are you doing here?" she asks into the telephone, stalling for time.

"I have to keep an eye on you, don't I?"

He won't look up!

"Just a moment," she says, "I'm helping someone Will you hold?"

"Of course."

She puts the phone down, runs as quietly as she can around the desk and across the room. Kenneth is young and strong, surely more than a match for him. "Kenneth," she whispers, "do me a favor."

"Sure, just give me a moment here."

"No! I'm sorry," she smiles at Kenneth's customer, "this is an emergency." She draws Kenneth away a few steps. "That man on the phone is making an obscene call. He's down the hall in the public phone booth. Will you—could you catch him for me?"

He looks at her, not sure if she is putting him on.

"Oh, please!"

"Sure, Miss Townsend. Hey, don't worry."

Katie looks around the room. "I don't know where any of the security guards are and there isn't time—"

"Hey, no sweat! Just tell me what he looks like."

"I don't *know* what he looks like!"

"Well, how will I know who he is?"

"He's in the phone booth! Right now!"

"*Which* phone booth?"

She catches her breath. In her excitement she has forgotten there is a whole line of booths. She motions Kenneth to come with her quietly. She goes back to her phone, lying on its side on the reference desk. She picks it up, listens. There is no dial tone. He has not hung up.

"Hello? Are you there?"

"Yes, my dear. Patient as Job."

"I mean *there.* Where you said."

"In the phone booth? Yes, dear child, I'm here. Do you want to come see me?"

"How will I know who you are?"

"I'm the only one in this booth."

"But *which* booth?"

"Oh, of course. The end booth, my dear, the one closest to the Arents Collection."

"The end booth?" she repeats for Kenneth's benefit. "Next to the Arents?"

Kenneth nods and takes off, running quickly and quietly in his jogging shoes.

"That's right," Charles says. "Will you come now to visit me?"

Silence. Katie watches Kenneth disappear around the corner of the entrance way. He'll be there in ten seconds.

"I don't know," she says. "I'm frightened."

She has to keep him talking. Would he hear the running feet?

"Frightened of me?"

"Yes."

"Of course you are. It's all my fault. I try to be nice to you, I *want* to be nice to you—"

It must be nearly ten seconds now. She listens, listens for the gasp, for the dropped receiver, for Kenneth's shouting voice—

"—but then I always seem to lose my temper, don't I? And then I play these little jokes on you. It's really not very nice of me, I know. But you're so tempting. Do you know how very tempting you are?"

"I—I know—"

"Do you? How very astute of you."

It *must* be ten seconds by now.

Any moment now—

"Katie? Are you there?"

"Yes, I'm here."

"But you're not allowed to receive personal calls at the library, are you? Perhaps I should hang up—"

"No!"

"No? And why so great a *no*, dear love?"

"I—"

"Yes? You—?"

Silence.

"I think I must go now."

"No! Don't!"

"Please?"

"Please."

"But why shouldn't I hang up? Could it be that you enjoy talking to me?"

Pause.

"Well then, if you don't, I'm sure I shouldn't be taking up so much of your time—"

"No! Don't go yet."

"Then you do enjoy talking to me?"

Pause.

"Yes."

"Say it, then. Say that you enjoy talking to me."

"I—I enjoy talking to you."

"Ask me to *please* talk to you."

"Yes. Please talk to me."

Kenneth appears in the doorway. Bewildered. He shrugs helplessly.

"You bastard!" she screams into the phone. "Where are you?"

He laughs.

All around the main reading room, heads lift and turn toward her. Hundreds of eyes stare at her in the broken silence.

And in the phone held to her ear, Charles is laughing.

She slams down the receiver.

Kenneth comes up to her. "Ain't nobody there," he says.

Her shoulders slump. She puts her hand to her eyes. She is shaking.

"You all right?" Kenneth asks.

She looks at him, takes a deep breath. "Yes," she says. "I'm all right. Wasn't there anybody there at all?"

"Nobody in any of the booths. Want to take a look for yourself?"

She walks with him down the long hallway. The phone booths are empty, all of them.

As they stand there, one of the phones rings.

She jumps. Looks at Kenneth.

He is puzzled.

It is the phone on the end that is ringing, the one closest to the Arents Collection.

Katie walks to it.

Lifts the receiver.

"Who knows?" the familiar, rasping voice says. "Who knows what evil lurks in the hearts of men? The Shadow knows!"

And then he chuckles, long and low and rasping, while she holds the receiver and tries very hard not to faint.

CHAPTER
2

Wally Gilford stood in front of the mirror shaving at five o'clock in the afternoon, trying to make himself pretty for the Widow Kellerman. He was feeling depressed.

Well, look, he tried to cheer himself up, you've got a right to be depressed. He had had a rotten conversation this afternoon with Dan Moller, the precinct captain. Wally had gone in to talk to him about the girl who had been found strangled in Howard Johnson's. It was over two weeks now, and Wally told the captain that he was filing the case.

"Nothing turned up, huh?"

Wally shook his head. "I'm about as convinced as I can be that there isn't anything that *can* turn up, there just *isn't* anything. She picked up a stranger, probably at Mcsorley's, and he killed her. Nobody there noticed him well enough to give anything useful in the line of a description, nobody at Howard Johnson's noticed them, and that's all there is to it."

"Nothing in her private life?"

"Nothing. I think we've found out all there is to find out about her, and there's nothing there. Like I say, I haven't bet on anything since Truman beat Dewey so I'm not putting any money on the table, but I'm as convinced as I can be that it was just some total stranger that done her in, as we say on the force."

Moller spread his hands. "Okay, what can I tell you? File it."

Wally hesitated. "You know what this means, don't you?"

"What? What's it mean?"

"Some guy picked her up out of nowhere, took her to the motel, there was no fight, nothing like that, he just quietly strangled her."

"So?"

"So we've got a nut loose out there."

"A nut? *A* nut? You're standing here kvetching because we've got one nut loose on the streets out there? Listen, Gilford, there are over nine million people in this goddamn city, you know that? Not counting the creeps from Connecticut who come in for the porno flicks, am I right? So I figure there is a minimum, and get this I say a *minimum*, of more than nine hundred thousand nuts loose out there on those streets every fucking day. Nine hundred *thousand* fucking nuts, and next year there'll be over a *million*. So don't stand there kvetching about one nut at Howard fucking Johnson's, for Christ's sake."

"I wouldn't argue with your statistics," Wally said, "but those nine hundred thousand nuts aren't all going around strangling people. This one is."

"I wish they would."

"What?"

"I wish the hell they would. I wish every one of those goddamn nine hundred fucking thousand nuts would go out there and strangle ten people a week. You know what I mean? With one in ten being a nut, at the end of a few weeks we'd get the nut population down to manageable proportions in this city. I could maybe even take a vacation. Visit the Statue of Liberty. Or the Empire State Building. You ever been up to the top of the Empire State, Gilford?"

"We could all take vacations," Wally said. "There wouldn't be anyone left alive in the whole damn city."

"That would suit me just fine," Moller said.

Well, a conversation like that would depress anybody. Wally sighed and stared in the bathroom mirror and rinsed the shaving lotion off his face. He didn't want to take the Widow Kellerman out to dinner tonight.

A lonely man could get by all right, he thought, if only he didn't have friends who insisted on fixing him up with lonely women. He wished he could sit home and read Trollope. *Phineas Finn* would be perfect for an evening like tonight, nothing to do, spend an hour cooking up something good, open a beer, relax . . . .

He put on a shirt and tied his tie. He'd probably be the only guy in the restaurant tonight wearing a tie. But the last time he had been to a restaurant with a woman everyone wore ties. That showed you how long ago it had been.

He sighed again, looked in the mirror, stuck out his tongue at himself, went to the closet, put on his coat and hat and walked out, locking both locks behind him.

He walked up Riverside to Ninety-fourth and turned right and found the Widow Kellerman's apartment building. He pulled open the door into the foyer, searched down the list of names, found her name, and pushed the button beside it.

He waited for her to buzz and let him into the building. He pushed his hat back on his head, took a deep breath, and stared into the street.

It was technically still daylight out there. If you stood in the middle of the street and craned your neck backward and looked straight up you could still see blue sky, but the tall buildings cut off the sun and the street was already dark. A city twilight.

Directly across the street was the entrance to another apartment building, similar but not identical to this one. The street had been empty when Wally walked up it, but now a young woman pushed a baby stroller up to the entrance and stopped in front of it. A paper shopping bag was wedged into the stroller beside her bundled child. It was cold out there.

She was bending now, lifting her child out of the stroller.

Wally watched her.

She was young, not beautiful but graceful. She held the keys in her mouth, her handbag tucked securely under the arm in which she now held the child on her hip as she reached down for the brown shopping bag.

It was all so natural, so lovely, that Wally found himself smiling as he rocked back on his heels watching her.

His view of the street was narrowed by the doors of the foyer in which he stood looking out, waiting for the Widow Kellerman to buzz the buzzer.

The young blond man appeared suddenly, moving into the edge of his field of vision.

The woman didn't see him; she was bending over the stroller, holding the baby perched on her left hip, reaching for the shopping bag, when he hit her viciously on the back of her head.

She lurched forward across the stroller, dropping the child. The child fell backward, arms flailing for one instant, striking the back of its head on the sidewalk. The mother fell forward, smashing her face on the sidewalk.

The man yanked her handbag from her shoulder as she fell and moved swiftly down the street.

It hadn't taken two seconds, and it was all over.

The man had already moved out of Wally's field of view. For another long second Wally stood there, paralyzed, shocked by the sudden violence that had broken a scene as peaceful as a Monet painting of a Sunday-afternoon picnic.

Then he ran out through the foyer door. Ran across the street past the woman who now began to scream. The baby was terribly quiet. Wally ran silently past them. He didn't stop to help, to comfort; he had no room in his heart for pity, he felt only a terrible rage. He ran after the man.

The man was walking swiftly. Wally didn't shout, he didn't want to frighten him into running, he wanted to catch him.

He was only five steps behind him now, four, three—

The man whirled.

Wally stopped.

As the man turned he whipped out a knife. It glinted now in the city twilight, picking up the light from the windows overhead.

He held it out in front of him. He smiled, sucking in breath noisily through his mouth.

"Give me your money, motherfucker," he said.

Wally reached under his overcoat and brought out his gun. He pointed it in the man's face.

"I *want* to shoot," he said. "So make a move."

He had never shot a man in his life. He had shot *at* men, but from a distance, and he had never hit them. He had never pointed a gun in a man's face and pulled the trigger. His hand was shaking.

The man dropped the knife.

"Up against the wall," Wally said. "Motherfucker."

He booked the mugger at the Nineteenth Precinct and then took a patrol car across town to Mount Sinai Hospital. In the emergency room they directed him to the third floor. Outside her room he found an upset young man.

As he had thought, the young man was her husband. "How is she?" Wally asked.

"She lost three front teeth and broke her nose. But that's nothing," he said sarcastically.

"If that's nothing, what's something?"

"She cracked something in her pelvis. They don't know if they'll have to operate to put in a pin, or what. She'll be here in this goddamn hospital for weeks. She may limp the rest of her life!"

"How's the baby?"

"Oh fine, just fine. *Only* a concussion."

"You going to press charges?"

"I'll kill that sonofabitch!"

"Will you press charges?"

"How am I going to take care of the baby? With her in the hospital for *weeks*? Christ, how am I gonna *pay* for it?"

"You want to come down now and press charges?"

"I have to go now?"

"Anytime in the next twenty-four hours will do. But now I can take you down in a patrol car and bring you right back."

The man took two quick steps away. "Christ!" he said. "Nobody cares, you know that? He could have killed her and the baby, too. And it happens every goddamn day in this city, you know that? And nobody cares!"

"I care."

"They don't prosecute, they plea bargain, you know what I mean?"

"I'll prosecute. I'll sit right on this one."

"Christ!"

He took short, quick steps up and down the hall. He stopped outside his wife's door, looking blankly at it.

"Is your wife sedated?" Wally asked.

He nodded.

"I'll have you back here before she comes out of it."

The man still hesitated. Wally put his hand on his shoulder. He shrugged it off angrily. "What's the point?" he asked.

"To take him off the streets, put him in jail where he belongs."

"Is that gonna help my wife?"

"I'm sure she'll want to see him punished for what he did."

"She's gonna want to see *me*! Me around the house, me taking care of the baby, me doing the cooking while she's laid up because of this bastard—"

"Let's put him away where he can't hurt anyone else—"

"I don't care about anyone else! I care about *me*! And her."

He walked away from Wally, three steps down the hall. He stopped and stood with his back to Wally, his shoulders hunched, trying to curl into a fetus in the hospital hallway.

"Don't you want to press charges?" Wally asked softly.

"Yes! Of course I want to! You don't understand."

"Tell me."

He began to mumble.

"I can't hear you," Wally said.

"I don't have the time! I got a job, you know what I mean? I can't run into court fifteen, twenty times—"

"It won't be fifteen times—"

"Whatever! I know how these things work, I read the papers."

Wally said nothing. He stood there and let him talk, hoping he'd talk his anger into action. But his words became quieter, slower, and finally dropped again into a mumble.

"What?" Wally asked.

"I don't want to ask for trouble."

"It's not that much trouble. You come down to the precinct, we type up the charges—"

"I don't mean that. I mean, like afterward? After the goddamn judge gives him ten days 'cause they talked the charges down to spitting on the sidewalk, after he gets out of jail, after he comes looking for us—"

"He's not going to come looking for—"

"Who's to stop him?! Even *before* he gets out of jail, he's got friends, don't he?"

"We can give you protection—"

"Ha!"

Wally went into the standard police line about protection for witnesses of violent crimes, but he knew and the young man knew that the protection can't go on forever. If you're really scared, the argument is not very convincing.

"What's the use?" the man asked softly. "What's

the point? You're angry now, you want to do something. I understand that, but you know the score just like I do. Even if they don't plea bargain down to nothing, he'll still be out on bond for months so what's to stop him coming after us? And even if they put him in jail he'll be out on parole in a year or two, so what's the whole fucking point? We got enough trouble, don't we? Just leave us alone."

Wally waited a few moments, then tried to make his voice as official as possible. "Will you come with me now to press charges?"

"No."

The man stood with his back to Wally, he wouldn't look at him. "I didn't see nothing," he said. "My wife didn't see who done it. We don't know nothing."

What is the point of it all?

Wally went home to his flat, and because he didn't want to indulge himself by soothing his anger with liquor, he settled for a beer. He sat down and drank the beer and wondered what the hell was the point of it all.

He should have killed that son of a bitch. He had the gun pointing right in his face and the punk was holding a knife, he should have pulled the trigger and blown his fucking face away.

Then there'd be a story in the papers tomorrow. Police brutality, the papers loved that. Kill one of these sons of bitches and everybody screams. Why don't they scream when these sons of bitches kill people, when they break faces and pelvises day after day after fucking goddamn day?

He should have killed the son of a bitch. Then maybe he wouldn't be trembling with anger now.

Christ, what a world. Jesus Christ, God Almighty, what a city.

He had finished the beer and it hadn't calmed him down at all. He poured a quick shot of scotch. He grimaced as he swallowed it. It wasn't the best stuff in the world. That punk mugger probably drinks Chivas Regal. Why not? When he wants some scotch, all he has to do is walk into a neighborhood liquor store and pull out his knife. He might as well take Chivas Regal as Harvey's.

He put the scotch away. There were few cops in this city who didn't end up drinking too much. He would settle for another beer. He opened the bottle and poured it carefully into a glass, sat down in his rocking chair and opened the book that lay on the table.

He was determined to find out what Anthony Trollope was all about. He sat there and drank his beer and read about Lady Glencora, and then after three pages he suddenly leaned forward and put his forehead down on the table and shook his head slowly from side to side.

He had just remembered the Widow Kellerman.

CHAPTER

3

"Maybe you should call the police?"

"I don't want to do that. Unless I have to. I will if I have to."

"Maybe you have to. Maybe it's time."

"I hope not."

"I know. It's a big step, isn't it?"

"It's an irrevocable step. I can call them in easily enough, but once I do I can't call them off. They'll want to know who is making the calls. They'll find out. They'll prosecute."

"Perhaps it would be simpler to change your phone number."

"No."

"You've already thought of that?"

"Of course I've thought of it. I won't do it. I'll call the police in first."

"You seem to feel strongly about it."

"I feel very strongly. It would be running away. It

would be admitting that my home has been invaded and that there's nothing I can do about it."

"Your home *has* been invaded. And what else *can* you do about it?"

"I don't know. But I won't run away. I promise you that. I'm not afraid."

"Yes you are."

Pause.

She looked out the kitchen window, holding the phone in her hand.

"You're afraid and I don't blame you," he said. "Who wouldn't be? A maniac calling you on the phone, shouting obscenities? Poor thing."

"Why do you do it?"

"Do it?"

"Why do you call me like this? Why are you so mean to me?"

"You don't understand. I don't mean to be. What are the words to that old song? 'I'm sure you don't mean to be, mean to me . . .' It's very complicated."

"Do you want to be my friend? Is that it? Are you the one who's afraid?"

"Me? Afraid?"

"I think perhaps you are."

"Why do you do it?"

"Me? *You're* the one making these calls!"

"That's not what I'm talking about. Why do you sleep with him?"

"With who?"

"That aging juvenile. The has-been actor. No, not has-been. He never was. And never will be. The *waiter*," he said contemptuously.

"How do you know about him?"

"I know everything. And it saddens me. A weak,

vacillating man, neither here nor there, how can you let his withering fingers touch your flesh, your breast, your—"

"He's not."

"Not?"

"Not as you describe him. He's a good man, he—"

"He is in disgrace with fortune and men's eyes. And can you find nothing more to say about him than that he is a *good* man? The weakest praise of all."

"You didn't let me finish—"

"What else could you say? When you first met him he must have been young and strong and glorious—"

"Yes, he was!"

"Was? *Was?*"

"That's not what I meant to say!"

"That's what you *did* say. He grows old, he grows old, it is disgusting for you to let him touch you. Promise me that you won't let him fuck you again."

"Don't talk like that!"

Pause.

"Never mind," he said softly, whispering, sadly. "Never mind. Do what you like. I don't care. I don't love you."

And he hung up.

"Maybe you should call the police?"

She smiled despite herself. "That's what *he* says."

"Who?"

"Charles. My friend on the phone."

"He told you to go to the police?" Peter asked.

She nodded.

He laughed. "He's got *chutzpah*, I'll say that for him. I know you don't like the fuzz, but what else can you do?"

"We used to call them pigs."

"We used to call them Officer Friendly."

"That was a long time ago."

"So was the *pigs* business. Anyway, what else can you do?"

"I don't know."

They were sitting on a wooden bench in the little park behind the library, with the pigeons to their left and Forty-second Street to their right. It was cold, but the sun had come out, and for a December day in New York City it was warm and balmy. Peter had brought sandwiches for their lunch and fresh steaming cups of coffee from the coffee and muffin stand on Sixth Avenue, and with the sun on their faces it was mild, soft and relaxing, pleasant.

"He's a maniac," Peter said.

"Sometimes he's not so bad. This morning he was just sad and lonely."

"And crazy. That's the most dangerous kind, Katie. One minute he's calm, the next minute he's raving. You never know what someone like that is going to do."

"I don't think there's any danger. I've been reading about him. I don't mean *him*, of course, I mean people like him. I spent my coffee break today in the psychology section—"

"Katie, don't get carried away because you once solved a murder. All the answers to everything aren't in that goddamned building of yours, they're not all written down in those fifty-seven million books. You need professional help. Go to the cops and tell them about it."

She sat and looked around the park. She threw the crust of her sandwich to the pigeons. Everything was so normal. It was only her phone that linked her to another world, a crazy world . . . .

"Maybe you're right."

She suddenly giggled. "I'll have to vacuum the apartment first," she said.

"Vacuum—?"

"Make sure there are no shreds of grass lying around."

"They're not going to be looking for grass."

"Of course they are! They always do. That would be just like them—someone calls them for help and they search out the apartment and arrest them for possession."

"Where do you get these ideas of yours?"

"They're not *ideas*," she said angrily, "they're memories! I remember Kent State—"

"That wasn't the police, that was the National Guard."

"They're all the same. And I remember Chicago."

"Chicago?"

"Chicago, 1968! Maybe you've forgotten, but I remember the cops smashing the skulls of a bunch of young kids who only wanted to stop the killing in Vietnam."

Peter sighed. "That was a long time ago," he said. "And a long way away."

"You think they've changed? It's even a longer time and a longer distance from Chicago 1968 to Berlin 1933, but the police behaved the same in both those places, didn't they? What makes you think they've changed now?"

"Maybe they haven't changed—"

"Maybe they haven't," she agreed.

"—but you have."

"Me?"

He smiled at her. "You, my love. In 1968 you were a long-haired kid with a cute little bottom, and you were chanting slogans and waving a sign that said 'Napalm the White House, not the green forests.' Today you're a middle-aged respectable lady librarian." He laughed. "I hate to be the one to tell you this, my love, but you've grown up."

She looked at him. He couldn't stop laughing.

"Have I?" she asked. She looked around sadly at the park, at the people on Forty-second Street, at the monstrous library looming behind them. She tried to remember the last time she had gone charging out into the streets with a sign and a cause. "Have I grown up?" she asked sadly. "Is that what's happened?"

"Maybe you should call the police?"

There! She had said it. Madame Szilardi bit her lip and wondered if she had gone too far. She hated to interfere in other people's lives, she really did, but what could one do when one *knew*?

The dream had been bad again.

Not exactly a dream. At least, when she had wakened in the morning she couldn't recall one particular dream, she couldn't remember being chased by vultures or being suffocated with a pillow or falling into a pit of wriggling snakes; she remembered only a feeling of terror.

So she had had two cups of black coffee to clean out her insides. She had drunk the coffee and walked around the room until she could feel it working, could feel her body becoming empty inside—it was silly, of course, she knew that her body wasn't really emptying because of the coffee, but that didn't matter. What mattered was the *feeling*, this *tuning* of her self into the cosmic consciousness.

Then she went to the bathroom.

Next she had to empty her mind. She sat at the piano and played a Bach cantata. Then she played it backwards.

Then she took a towel from the linen closet and spread it on the kitchen table. She put exactly nine ice cubes on it, folded it back over the ice cubes, and rolled up the ends. She carried it into the living room and lay down on the couch.

The curtains were still drawn and the room was quite dark. The sun must have been up by then, but here in her Fifth Avenue flat with western exposure it was still dark.

She lay down on the couch, leaned her head back, and closed her eyes. She placed the ice-packed towel over her forehead.

She could hear nothing.

She could see nothing.

She was aware only of the moist coolness on her brow.

She waited for the world to recede, for the universe to dissolve into the dark, cool, moist weight.

Little by little it did.

She felt the house go first. She felt the universe shrink down to this one room, and then the walls of the room, too, were gone. In the whole universe there were now only she and the couch and the cool towel.

And finally the couch dissolved.

She was left floating in the void, in eternity, in cool moist emptiness, alone with the universe.

She floated, unthinking, undreaming.

And then suddenly her hands clapped together. She

sat bolt upright. Her eyes popped open. She stared into the dark room. The universe reeled about her, flooded in on her.

The face she saw was Katie's.

The terror she felt was Katie's.

And then the vision faded away into the reeling universe. She endured without complaint the vertigo, the nausea, which had to come, which always came. And then finally the universe began to slow, the house swirled and spun around her more and more slowly, finally it came to rest and she was back again.

Gingerly she stood up. She was dizzy and nearly fell. She took ten deep breaths. Then she carried the towel into the kitchen, emptied the remains of the ice cubes into the sink, wrung the towel out and hung it over the faucet to dry.

There was no doubt left in her mind. She had suspected it from the beginning and now she was sure. Katie was in a terrible danger.

There was no question of that, the question was how could she help?

She made herself a bowl of porridge and sat down to eat it and to think.

What was the danger? She didn't know.

Did Katie know?

She stirred the porridge and stared into it.

She had to talk to Katie, that was obvious.

But it was so awkward. She didn't want Katie to think she was interfering; young people are so sensitive to that. And they are so insensitive to danger. Why else do they neglect to fasten their seatbelts, and ride motorcycles, and smoke marijuana and cigarettes and the Lord knows what else these days?

She needed a pretext. Some little reason to call Katie

on the phone casually and arrange a meeting, something completely ordinary, completely unpremeditated.

She washed out her bowl and the pot in which she had cooked the porridge. She went back into the living room and drew the drapes—and was struck between the eyes by a dazzling glare of whiteness.

She blinked. The brown, faded grass of Central Park had been covered with a white blanket. It had snowed during the night. How delightful! The whiteness was dazzling, vibrant, beautiful.

It was queer. Only yesterday the sun had been shining and the weather had been warm and balmy. And now, look, during the night a cold wind must have traveled down from the Arctic, the temperature must have plummeted, and the snow had come down from heaven to coat this imperfect world.

It was destiny, she thought. On the streets of the West Side the snow would be turned into black sooty slush by now; it would be a dirty nuisance. But over here on Fifth Avenue, the Central Park vistas were a vision of loveliness, a perfect reason to invite Katie over for the day.

Because the library was open Saturdays, the staff had Sunday and one floating day off each week. With any luck at all, Katie's day off would be today or tomorrow. In fact, it was nearly a fifty-fifty chance that it would be. And so Madame Szilardi went right to the phone and called Katie and told her how beautiful it was and asked if she could possibly take the day off to come and see it. And today did happen to be her day off, and yes, the idea of walking in Central Park sounded perfectly delightful. It was just the thing she needed, Katie said; she needed to get away from the city hassle for a day.

And so right after breakfast she caught the M-18 crosstown bus, and Madame Szilardi met her at Eighty-fourth Street. Katie was wearing her high boots, Madame Szilardi her rubber galoshes, and they went for a tramp through the park, through the virgin snow and the clean, brilliant air.

They talked very little on the walk; they returned slightly out of breath from climbing the hill back to Fifth Avenue, stripped off their boots and galoshes and heavy coats, and then sat down for a cup of hot tea. Madame Szilardi toasted muffins and set out marmalade and preserves and three different cheeses, and they finally sat down and relaxed and began to talk.

Madame Szilardi had been wondering how to bring up the subject of danger without seeming to be an interfering bore when Katie said, out of the blue, "You know, I've been getting obscene phone calls."

That was it, then. Madame Szilardi knew at once, this was the danger. "Tell me all about it, my dear," she said, her eyes glistening with excitement as she bit into the delicious toasted muffin dripping with strawberry preserves. A thousand calories, at least, she thought defiantly, and to hell with it. "Tell me everything."

And Katie did. When she had finished, Madame Szilardi nodded once or twice, looked as seriously as possible at her, and took the bit between her teeth. "Maybe you should call the police?" she suggested.

"Do you think I should?"

"Yes, I do. I know you're skeptical of the other world, but in fact the reason I called you today was not to show you the snow but to tell you of the messages I've been receiving."

"What messages, precisely?"

"Well, you know they're not *precise* at all. It is, after all, more an art than a science. That's why I've been hesitating about bringing it up. But the import is clear. I ask you to believe me when I say this: You are in terrible danger, my dear. And I'm sure it has something to do with these awful phone calls, with this despicable man who is haunting you."

"But he's not despicable. Sometimes—"

"Yes?"

"Sometimes he's almost sweet. He's sick, of course. He's sad and lonely, but he doesn't want to hurt me. He's asking for help."

Madame Szilardi shook her head. "No, my dear," she said, "you are quite wrong. He does want to hurt you."

"I missed you yesterday."

Katie closed her eyes. She held the phone and closed her eyes and bit her lip and was silent. She would not answer him. She would not talk to him.

It had been lovely yesterday at Madame Szilardi's, lovely because of the snow and the cozy flat and the sweet old lady herself, who was such a dear, and it had been lovelier still because she had known she was free at least for the day from this. For that reason, when Madame Szilardi asked her, she had stayed the night and had gone in early this morning, directly to work. So she had had two whole days free of this man, but now here he was again.

"I missed you," he said again. "Where did you go? Do you think you can escape me?"

She would not say a word, not one word.

He was silent. He waited.

She broke. "Don't you have anyone else to call up and make nasty remarks to?" she asked.

"You weren't with him."

"With who?"

"The has-been."

"How do you know?"

"I know everything."

"You don't know where I was yesterday!"

Pause. "You're right. I don't know where you were yesterday. And yesterday night. Who were you sleeping with?"

"I don't have to tell you."

"I'll find out. You can't hide from me. I am always there, I follow you everywhere—"

"Why?!"

"Because I love you."

Pause.

"You said last time that you didn't love me."

"I don't. Do, don't. Yes, no. Black, white. Higgledy piggledy, my white hen, she lays down for gentlemen."

"It seems a strange sort of love."

"Yes. What can I tell you?"

"You sound so sad."

"I am sad. I'm hurt."

"Why?"

"Because you slept with another man last night."

"I didn't. I slept alone—"

"Don't lie to me!"

Pause.

"Do you really expect me to be faithful to a strange voice on the telephone that calls to make obscene and frightening remarks?"

"I don't mean to frighten you. I'm sorry. It's just

that I want to fuck you so very badly. And there you are, going to bed with everyone else."

"Instead of calling like this," she said, taking a deep breath to swallow her fright, "why don't you come over and talk to me face to face? This can't be good for you, you know, hiding like this."

"Will you let me in?"

"Yes."

"Is he there?"

"Who?"

"The man you slept with last night."

"There's no one here."

"Maybe you want him to see me, as a witness. And then you'll call the police."

"No. I want to help you."

"Shall we let him watch while we fuck?"

"You mustn't talk like that."

"All right. I won't. But shall we?"

"No."

"We shan't let him watch?"

"We're not going to—"

"What? We're not going to what?"

"We're not going to fuck!"

He laughed. "Now you're using obscene language to me. We're making progress, aren't we?"

"No!"

"Oh dear, I thought we were."

"Won't you come to see me instead of talking to me like this?"

"I don't *want* to talk to you like this," he said, sad again.

"I know."

"I don't want to see you, either."

"What do you want?"

He laughed again. "You know what I want. I think you like to hear me say it, don't you?"

"No."

"I want to fuck you. I also want to kill you."

"No." Softly. "Please, no." Almost a whimper.

"Yes. Little pinpricks of pain as I put my hands around your throat and squeeze—"

She hung up then.

And, shaking, called the police.

CHAPTER

4

The Law is the Embodiment
 Of all that's Good and Excellent;
It has no possible fault or flaw,
 And the Police of New York embody
 the Law.

W.S. Gilbert said something roughly
like that, and he was absolutely right. In these days of
rampant crime and corruption, it is good to remember
that when the savages are breaking down the last
barriers, the United States Cavalry—dressed in blue,
with New York Police Department shields pinned
proudly to their chests—are still alive and riding to
the rescue. They are indeed New York's Finest.

"And I," said Wally Gilford, "am Marie of
Rumania."

"What?" asked Nicely-Nicely.

"I said, I am Marie of Rumania. I was just reading

this article in the *Times*. About the department. You read it?"

"Why would I want to read anything the *Times* has to say about the department?"

"You've got something there."

"Why did you say you were what's-her-name?" asked Nicely-Nicely.

"Marie of Rumania. It's an expression. Like in the Dorothy Parker poem."

"Who's Dorothy Parker?" Nicely-Nicely asked.

Wally looked at him with a pained expression, then silently put his head down on his desk and said no more. Nicely-Nicely didn't even notice. He went back to his typing.

Nicely-Nicely was Detective Albert Annunciato, and he was called Nicely-Nicely because he insistently objected to being called Fat Albert and because he looked like the actor Stubby Kaye, who played Nicely-Nicely Johnson in *Guys and Dolls*. Nobody in the division knew why the character in the play was called Nicely-Nicely. Nobody read Damon Runyon anymore. Let alone Dorothy Parker.

It was nearly the end of the four P.M. to midnight shift, and they were the only detectives left in the squad room. They heard the noises of the relief crew outside, but so far none of them had appeared in the room; they weren't yet officially there. Wally had just come back in from a burglary call. He had managed without much effort to convince the occupants of the apartment—who were old and cynical New Yorkers, who knew the score—that there wasn't any point going through the motions of an official investigation; it would just be wasting their time and his. There were, after all, over two hundred thousand burglaries in New York in 1980, and there aren't enough cops in all the Western democracies put together to investigate that many burglaries. So the fact that there were less than twenty thousand burglary arrests in 1980 is understandable.

The Nelkins, the burgled couple, could understand that. They would settle, they said, for the police slip which confirmed that a burglary had been committed and that it had been dutifully reported to the police, without which no insurance company was obliged to make compensation.

Nicely-Nicely was typing an arrest report on a husband-wife assault. Wally was wondering whether to attempt filing the papers that littered his desk or throw them away. If he threw them away, at least one of them would become very important tomorrow. But they were weeks and months old and he no longer remembered how to file them. It was a tough decision.

The phone rang.

Nicely-Nicely looked at Wally.

Wally looked back and smiled.

It was nearly twelve. They were nearly off duty. But the ringing phone might be summoning one of them to a new case that would last many more hours before whoever answered it could go home.

Nicely-Nicely looked again at Wally, and Wally smiled right back at him. Because it was Nicely-Nicely's turn to answer the phone.

He sighed, and picked it up.

Wally decided to postpone his decision about the accumulated litter on his desk in favor of finishing the *Times*. He listened with only half an ear to Nicely-Nicely's whine on the telephone, which soon carried an air of relief as he realized the caller had one of those problems that can be put off, and that he would not be called out once more on this shift to brave the cold air and perilous night of the city.

The *Times* said that nuclear radiation was bad. Well, that made sense, Wally thought. But it didn't go into the question of whether coal dust was good, or if there was any alternative at all that wasn't worse.

All they want to do is sell papers, Wally thought. Nobody gives a damn for anything else. Just sell your goddamn papers.

"Right, lady," Nicely-Nicely was saying. "You got a problem, I would be the last person in the world to deny that. What I am saying is, this is not the kind of problem we can do much about. Do you understand what I'm saying? 'Cause you see, lady, there are what, eight or ten million people in this city? So maybe three million of them are kooks and it only costs ten cents to make a phone call, obscene or whatever, and it's probably even tax deductible if you get a good lawyer.

"Yeah, lady, I know. Everybody thinks it's easy to trace a call but no, lady, it is not; it is pretty damned near impossible and what with the Supreme Court and all—What? Well, you see, they've put so many restrictions on anything like this that the paper work involved to set up a trace is like you wouldn't believe, believe me. Oh, you read the *Anderson Tapes*? Did you also read where it says right on the front page that it's a novel? You know what a novel is, lady? It means it's fiction, made up, fairy tales—Oh, I didn't know that. No, you didn't say. Right, you're a librarian, you know what a novel is. And you're upset about these calls, I can understand that, but, lady, I'm a cop and I'm telling you what is what, right?"

Dorothy Parker. Wally bet that if he asked everyone in the district there wouldn't be two cops that would know who Dorothy Parker is. Was. In fact, if all the cops in New York were laid end to end—

"—So even if we could set up a trace, which with the paper work involved is like just not gonna happen in this world for something like an obscene caller unless you're maybe Margaret Thatcher or Golda Meir—even if we could set it up, the guy if he has any sense at all is calling from a coin box so what are we gonna do about it really, lady, huh? You know what I mean? Why not just change your number or leave the phone off the hook? These guys get discouraged very easy. What? Well, you know, I wouldn't really call that a threat against your life. It sounds more like an afterthought, wouldn't you say? Obscene, I grant you, this is certainly an obscene caller, but threatening? I don't think you can call that really threatening. That's just the one time he ever said anything like that, right? You know what I think? I think he probably scared himself when he said that and you're never gonna hear from him again, that's what I think. Now you just go to sleep and forget about it, huh?"

Twelve o'clock.

Wally crumpled up the *Times* and dropped it in the wastebasket.

The door opened and the first of the midnight-to-eight-A.M. shift ambled reluctantly in.

Nicely-Nicely looked anxiously up at the clock. He was officially off duty now, and the department was not about to pay overtime for talking to frightened librarians.

"Yeah, I'm sure it's gonna be all right, miss. I tell you what, if these calls don't stop in two, three weeks,

you call right back and we'll see what we can do—
Well yeah, to be honest, I gotta tell you there's not
gonna be much that we can do, even then. But, you
know, the phone company's very good about changing
your number. If you want, you can tell them I
suggested it. They won't give you no hassle, I can
guarantee that. Okay, lady, have it your way. Sure,
you're very welcome. And have a good night."

"Buy you a cup of coffee?" Wally asked.

Nicely-Nicely shook his head, hanging up and
reaching for his coat and hat. "Thanks, but I gotta get
home. My old lady gets nervous, alone in the apartment at night, you know what I mean? See you
tomorrow."

"I hope I'm not a nuisance. I was just wondering if
you had any more problems? You know what I mean."

Katie smiled and sat up in bed. She yawned into the
receiver.

"Oh dear, did I wake you?" Madame Szilardi asked.
"I hope not. What time is it? I was just so worried, you
see. I had a precognition—no, not *exactly* a precognition, I don't want you to think I'm putting on airs, just
a *feeling* that he might have called again—"

"It's all right, Madame Szilar—"

"Cynthia."

"Cynthia, it's all right. I had just awakened," she
lied. "And you're right, he did."

"I absolutely knew it, I could *feel* it, do you see?
Was he very nasty?"

"As a matter of fact, he was."

"Now you simply must speak to the police, dear. I
am going to insist—"

"As a matter of fact, I have."

"—you cannot allow this to continue any longer. The man may be dangerous. There's no telling what that sort of—what did you say?"

"I said that I did phone the police. Late last night, after he called."

"My dear, I am so relieved! That'll be the end of it now, you'll see. What did they say?"

"Nothing at all. And I'm glad of it."

She nodded to herself. Yes, she was glad of it. Her room looked so different in the calm light of day. Last night the bureau threw a dark shadow in the lamp-light, a shadow that seemed to move whenever she glanced away from it, while her terrified mind threw dark shadows everywhere, shadows that slunk and snuck up on her whenever she turned her back. . . . It was all very different in the light of day. She was glad the policeman had pooh-poohed her fears. He had been right.

"Oh dear," said Madame Szilardi. "Didn't he believe you?"

"He believed me. But he said that such people aren't dangerous. They get their kicks out of the phone call, and that's the end of it."

"I dare say, in the usual scheme of things. But—and I don't want to alarm you, but I must say this—I feel this is different. You'll remember I said so right from the beginning, right from the very moment I met you on our television program. That's when it started, right at that moment, I know it. Oh dear, what shall we do? Did you tell him—the policeman—about me? About my—*feeling?*—that there is a real danger?"

Katie hesitated. "No," she said. "I don't want to hurt your feelings, but you know what his reaction would be."

"Only too well. Yes, policemen are very skeptical.
No matter how many crimes one helps them solve,
they never seem to be able to get the knack of actually
believing. You were absolutely right not to mention
me, I understand perfectly. The question now is, what
shall we do?"

"Nothing."

"I beg your pardon?"

"Nothing. I don't want to do anything. I just want to
forget about it."

"But—"

"Madame—Cynthia. You must understand. The
police know about these things. They're profession-
als."

Madame Szilardi winced. That hurt her pride. What
was she, an *amateur*? But one doesn't say these things.
"I know how you feel" is what she said.

Only that, and nothing more.

If I am for myself alone, the Bible tells us, of what
good am I?

Damn the torpedoes, the history books tell us, full
speed ahead!

And I have not yet begun to fight!

And when the going gets tough, the tough get going.

And fools walk in where angels fear to tread.

No, that last one doesn't fit. Somewhere, Madame
Szilardi thought, I seem to have got on the wrong
track. Now how did it go? Damn the torpedoes, that's
right, and full speed ahead!

She walked up the steps into Manhattan North and
asked for the precinct captain.

An hour and a half later, Captain Moller was saying,
"Who? What's a Madame Szilardi, Sergeant? And why
do you think I would want to see her?"

"I don't know what she is, sir, but where she's from is from NBC."

"She's from what?"

"NBC, sir. You know, the television network?"

"My God. She's from NBC, and she's been waiting *how* long? Bring her in!"

And so Madame Szilardi was ushered into the office to find Captain Moller on his feet, greeting her with outstretched arms, escorting her to a chair, and asking what the police forces of New York City could do for her.

"I hardly know how to begin," she began, "and I suppose that's the standard beginning. It would help if you had seen me on television a few weeks ago?"

The captain smiled apologetically.

"Of course," Madame Szilardi said graciously. "It was taped, of course, and shown in the morning. You must have been at work."

"Time and tide, you know—"

"Of course. I shall have to explain, then." But not about herself. She understood full well how a revelation of her extrasensory powers was likely to be greeted by the New York police.

So she told him merely that she had appeared recently on a morning talk show with Miss Katherine McGregor Townsend, a librarian of this city, who had told the nationwide television audience (Nielsen rating, 17.8) of her success in helping several police departments solve crimes—

"I don't want to appear rude, Madame Szilardi, but the New York Police do not need amateur help. We're grateful for—"

"You misunderstand, Captain. I am not here to offer her services, but to beg yours. Miss Townsend has been receiving obscene and threatening phone calls."

Captain Moller pulled a pad of paper across the desk, placed it in front of him, picked up a pen and said, "Tell me all about it."

Thirty minutes later she had done so and had left with the captain's assurance of prompt action ringing hearteningly in her ears, and Captain Moller was sitting again at his desk, with his head hanging heavily in his hands.

What does God have against me? he wondered. Why is it always me?

He stood up, walked to the door of the squad room, and opened it. It was just four o'clock. The shift was changing.

Wally Gilford was the first man of the four-to-midnight to come into the room.

"Gilford!" Captain Moller called. "You take a call last night from some dame getting obscene calls?"

Wally shook his head.

"Late last night," Captain Moller insisted, "must have been eleven-thirty, twelve, maybe after twelve."

"If it was after twelve it wasn't my shift—"

"I know that, I know that! I'm asking if you took the call, that's all."

"Not me. Maybe Nicely-Nicely, he took a call just before we left, it sounded like he was calming someone down."

"Nicely-Nicely. What's he working on?"

"That kid that got thrown off the roof yesterday. The girl who was raped outside the Natural History. And that girl who was knifed, raped, and tortured on West End. And, let me think, oh yeah the old woman—"

"Yeah, never mind. What you working on? No, don't tell me. Come in the office."

Why *me*, Lord God of Hosts? Wally asked silently. He followed his captain into the office and sat down and heard about Miss Townsend's troubles.

"So what do you want me to do?" he asked.

"What do I want you to do? How about finding the creep?"

"Impossible."

They stared at each other.

"Nicely-Nicely was right," Wally said. "All you can do is calm the girl down. You know that. So what's the fuss?"

"Do you ever listen to me? Does anyone around here ever listen to me? I know I'm only the captain of this precinct and that doesn't mean much and I hate to bother you guys—"

"I listened to you."

"You listened to me?"

"Yes."

"And did you hear me? I mean, you did *hear* me? The *words*? They were English words, weren't they? There are still some people around this city who speak English, aren't there? Should I maybe speak Spanish? You do still understand English?"

"I understand English. You split a compound verb."

"What?"

"A compound verb. *Do understand.* One shouldn't split compound verbs. Not as solecistic as splitting an infinitive, but—"

"Gilford, do me a favor? Would you go off somewhere where you won't be arrested for obscene behavior in public and take a flying fuck at yourself?"

Wally nodded. "Anything else?"

"Yes, there's something else. As long as you're here, would you just *listen* to me? Did I or did I not tell you that this broad was on television a couple of weeks ago telling the whole fucking world that she's gonna catch some murderer? Now look at it this way, Gilford: What if this guy's that killer? The guy calling her, I mean. What if he's after her?"

"Crap."

"But what if? What if the television networks pick up on this story about the broad catching killers and then being threatened? Sounds like a good story, right?"

"What do I know? I'm only a dumb—"

"*I* know! It's exactly the stupid kind of story they like! And if they pick up on it they're gonna want to know what the fuck the New York Police Department is doing about it! So now you know."

"Now I know."

"So *do* something about it. Go talk to the broad. In person, not on the phone. Tell her—I don't know what to tell her. Do something."

Wally stood up.

"You know why he's doing this?" Captain Moller asked.

"Who, the obscene caller?"

"No, not him. God. You know why God is doing this?"

Wally shook his head.

"Because I retire in two years," Captain Moller told him. Wally looked doubtful. Captain Moller nodded his head forcefully. "That's why," he insisted. "In two years I retire on full captain's pension. God's trying to fuck me out of it. He's going to make something happen to this broad and the television networks will pick up on it and dump on my head. They're gonna ask why the New York Police Department didn't do something to protect this girl. You mark my words, Gilford, she's gonna get her goddamn throat cut and I'm gonna get fucked out of my pension. God doesn't like policemen. That's why he made Puerto Ricans."

Wally turned to go.

"Gilford," Captain Moller said. "Do something."

Wally nodded. "So help me God," he said.

CHAPTER

5

Wally stood on Fifth Avenue, looking up at the two stone lions guarding the steps. Well, he thought, let's get it over with and get back to some real work. She had said when he called her that she'd be getting off duty at five, even though the library was open till nine tonight.

He sighed as he climbed the steps. Public relations and politics, that's what police work was all about. Here he was in a city swamped and drowning in murders, robberies, muggings and rapes, going to spend an hour with a frightened librarian because the captain was afraid someone on TV would make an unkind remark.

And why was she frightened? An obscene phone call. Probably some guy dialed the wrong number and when she answered he said, "Oh, shit," and hung up.

He went through the revolving doors into the

massive stone entrance hall. He checked his coat and hat. There were two gigantic flights of steps on either side of the enormous room. No wonder she was jumpy. The library wasn't Gothic, architecturally speaking, but it was decidedly gothic in the imaginary sense. Like an ancient stone haunted castle. Take this large empty room to begin with, you know what Freud said the mind subconsciously symbolizes as large, empty rooms. Some of our most frightening dreams take place there.

He climbed the flight of steps along the wall and stood for a moment on the balcony, looking down. What a place to work. What a great place for a murder. He imagined what Hitchcock could have done with this place.

She had said she'd be on duty in the main reading room on the third floor. He walked down the long, cold, stone hallway and found the crisscrossing steps to the third floor. He imagined working here late at night or early in the morning, when it wasn't crowded with people. Eerie, certainly. Frightening, even. The haunted library. He could almost believe it himself. Funny, when you looked at it like this, how different it seemed from the crowded, bustling place it now was. The reality of the world inside is a totally different reality.

Wally could imagine what life must be like for her. Leaving a cold, empty apartment every morning to come here to this cold, empty, haunted house. The high ceilings, long hallways, twisting stairs, massive cold stone. And then returning at night to the cold, empty, always empty flat. Poor lady. It was no fun living alone in New York, or anywhere else for that matter. No fun at all, he told himself, and never realized that he was talking about himself. Poor lady librarian.

He found the third-floor reading room. He stood just inside the doorway, making the scene from habit, aware that these people are not those who generally flesh out his days. It had been a long time since he had visited the library; it was easier to pick up a paperback. He had forgotten how much he had always liked the place.

The information desk was in the middle of the room, and there were three people working it, a young black man, an elderly lady, and a strikingly lovely young lady. He guessed the elderly woman was his, and got in her line. As he waited, he noticed that the line leading to the lovely young lady was longer than the other two, and that most men naturally joined it nevertheless.

He watched her as he waited, moving slowly forward in his line. She radiated youth—he found himself thinking of the phrase, the glory of youth, and wondered where it had come from—and yet she wasn't really young. She was certainly older than his daughter; she wasn't a pretty kid, she was a gorgeous woman. He realized with a sudden shock that she must be about the age his wife would be today.

He grimaced ruefully. He supposed he would never have another woman. If his daughter doesn't get in the way, his wife does. He couldn't even lech after a woman properly. But he was happy to see the men getting into the lovely lady's line, despite the longer wait.

"Can I help you?"

"Oh. Sorry. Daydreaming. Miss Townsend?" he asked the older woman.

She turned to her left, turned unbelievably to the lovely young thing. "Katie, this gentleman wants you."

Katie smiled brightly and questioningly, and with great presence of mind, Wally thought to say, "Uh."

"I beg your pardon?"

"Uh, my name is Gilford. I called you a half-hour ago."

"Oh. Yes." She glanced around. "I'll be finished in just a few minutes. Can you wait?"

He found an empty chair at one of the long, wooden tables and waited. He was the only one sitting there who stared at the librarian.

She finished at five and took him into the staff room. She brought them each a cup of coffee and they sat down. "Now then," she said, "I don't understand what this is all about."

"Didn't you call the police last night, complaining about a threatening call?"

"Yes. Did I talk to you?"

"No."

"Well, the officer I talked to explained that there isn't very much you can do about it. So why are you here now? In fact," she asked with a sudden frown of suspicion, "how do you know my name?"

"What?"

"My name!"

"Didn't you leave it last night?"

"No! He never asked my name!"

She dropped the cup of coffee. The cup fell to the floor and broke. The coffee splashed over their legs. Katie didn't notice. She was backing away from him. "Who are you?" she asked.

"Detective Wallace Gilford—"

"No you're not! The police don't know my name. You're *him*."

They were alone in the staff room, but there was the noise of people right outside. She was in no danger, but Wally could see she was terrified. She wasn't just a lonely woman trying to get attention, she was scared.

He held out his wallet, open to the gold badge and his identity card. "Look at the picture," he said. "That's me."

She took it from him. "I don't believe you," she said.

"Look, you can call the precinct and ask the sergeant on duty if they have a Detective Gilford there. He'll tell you. Then I'll get on the phone and ask him to identify my voice to you. Or we can even go there right now if you like. Okay?"

She wavered. "How do you know who I am?" she asked.

"This afternoon some woman from the television network came to see the captain. She explained the whole story."

"No. No one knows about it. No one but Peter and Madame—" She stopped. She fell back into her chair with relief. "She did it. I know she did."

"Madame—?"

"Szilardi. A friend of mine. We were on the program together. I bet she did it."

"Okay. Now let's check me out by phone."

"No, it's all right. I'm sorry, it was just—"

"I don't want you to have any doubts. You look up the number of the precinct in the phone book and call them yourself and we'll get me positively identified, okay?"

When they had done that, they sat down again and

Wally took out his notebook and said, "Now tell me all about it."

"All right," she said. "And look, I'm sorry. It's just that I'm nervous and I suddenly realized you don't look like a policeman."

"I don't?"

"Well, how I expected a policeman to look. Oh God, I'm being silly."

"What did you expect?"

"I hadn't thought of it. But I guess I think of cops as caricatures. You know, the whole bit, Irish, big jaw, thick neck, big cigar—"

"Big feet."

"I'm sorry."

"You don't have a high opinion of cops."

"No."

They looked at each other.

"No, I don't," she said again, screwing up her courage to say it, but why should she hide her feelings? "I remember too many things."

"Chicago?"

She was surprised. She nodded.

"Alabama?"

She nodded again.

"Serpico?"

"Yes! I don't trust you."

"Me?"

"All cops!"

Pause.

"I'm sorry," she said. "That's how I feel. You want me to be honest, don't you?"

"Not particularly. I think I'd rather you were polite."

"Look, I'm sorry—"

"Why don't we just skip all this? Just tell me what the problem is, and let's not worry if you like cops or not."

She hadn't known policemen were so sensitive. What had she said, actually? *He* was the one who brought up Chicago and Alabama—oh, the hell with it! She had her own problem to worry about. So she told him about the calls, and about the TV program, and about the man she had talked about, who she thought might have murdered two wives.

He wrote it all down and then sat there, thinking about it, not looking at her. On purpose not looking at her, she realized. She *had* been a bitch. He had a nice face. He *didn't* look like a cop, and she knew what she meant even though she couldn't express it. It wasn't such a terrible thing to think; he didn't look like a businessman either, or a barber or a politician. He looked intelligent and sensitive, like a director or maybe a lighting designer. She wished she hadn't hurt his feelings, saying that about cops—

She suddenly thought about something else. "What are you doing here, anyway?" she asked him.

"I told you—"

"You said Madame Szilardi told your captain just what I explained to someone else last night. So last night I was told there wasn't anything to be done, not to make a fuss. So how come today we're making a fuss?"

Wally shrugged.

"It couldn't be because she mentioned the television program, could it?"

"Could be."

"Could be. I'll just bet!" She was *really* angry now. Here he had her feeling sorry for him, apologizing for saying nothing but what she had always known was true. She was sitting around with him, thinking that maybe all cops weren't like she knew they were, and all the time the only reason he was here was because they were worried maybe the television would say something nasty about them. "Let's get it absolutely straight," she said. "Last night I called the cops to say somebody was threatening my life, and the answer was to get lost, sister!"

"Not exactly—"

"Exactly! That's *exactly* what I was told. And today, when you find out there might be a television connection, *then* you're all solicitous and John Wayne and Officer Friendly! Would you say that's a fair summary?"

Wally snapped his notebook shut. "Look, you called us for help. Now, you want it or not?"

"Not! Forget the whole thing!"

"That suits me just fine!" He stood and turned his back. But he didn't leave. Why, God, he thought, why *do* You hate policemen?

He turned back to her. "You can't call the cops in and then call us off when your feelings get hurt. We're in, so forget how we got in and just sit back and shut up and listen to me. I'm going to check out this guy you told me about and the two wives you *think* he murdered, but my guess is there's nothing to that. Your creep is probably some nut who knows you from the library—"

"Someone on this staff? With the words he's using? You must be out of your mind—"

"I didn't *say* someone on the staff! Probably one of the unwashed masses yearning to breathe free that you feel so strongly about from Chicago. He probably saw you on the TV and somehow that flipped his lid, since all this started right after that."

"What's going to happen?" she asked despite herself.

He shrugged. "Probably nothing. Probably he'll call a few more times and finally get bored and go away. The only thing I don't like is this feeling you say you have of there being a progression to the calls, like he's changing a bit each time."

"You think maybe he's working himself up to do something?"

"No, I don't think that. *You* think that."

She shrugged, very tough.

Well hell, he thought, relenting just a bit, it would scare him too. He dug into his wallet and found a card with his name and phone number on it. "If he calls again and gives you the impression of a *real* threat, if he scares you, call me. I'll come right over—I don't live too far from you."

She stared at the card he was holding out to her. She wanted to take it, but . . . "I'm not afraid of him," she said. "He doesn't scare me."

"*If* he scares you. If not, don't call."

She shrugged, and inside, angry as he was, he very nearly laughed. So *tough*. So tough, and so scared. "Any time," he said. "Cops don't sleep. He calls you, you call me."

She took the card. She kept her eyes down.

He seldom gave anyone his home phone number. It wasn't smart to get involved. He didn't know why he gave it to her, to a broad who hated cops.

She held the card. She stared at it, not really seeing it, just staring at it to keep from looking up. She watched his feet turn away and walk toward the door.

She *was* a bitch, she thought. It wasn't *his* fault.

She looked up just as he was leaving. "Mr. Gilford," she called.

He turned around at the door.

"Thank you," she said, and smiled.

And he felt very funny. He nodded, puzzled, and walked out.

CHAPTER
6

The phone rings.

Katie is asleep. Automatically, without thinking, she reaches out and grabs it to stop the sudden noise. She lifts it, not yet really awake. "Hello."

Silence.

She is awake now. Alone in the dark. And vulnerable and frightened. "Hello!"

Silence.

She closes her eyes. Breathes deeply. If she hangs up, he will only ring again. She holds the phone quietly and waits.

Finally a whisper.

"I'm coming to get you. You will feel my fingers around your throat."

Involuntarily she gasps, "No!"

Silence.

And then again the hoarse whisper. "Tonight."

She clutches the phone.

Softly—*click*—he hangs up.

And is gone.

Gone—where?

She looks out the window, out to where the weak streetlamps illumine the night but do not dispel it. The dark is enveloping. He is out there. And he is coming. Tonight.

She turns on the bed-table light. It is three o'clock in the morning. She jumps out of bed and turns on all the lights. She runs to the door and checks all the locks.

Not enough.

She runs to each window, locking them all. She stands, then, out of breath, looking around her barricaded fortress. She sees that now she is cut off from the outside world. And not safe at all. For windows can be broken, doors can be forced. If only he would call again, at least then she would know he is not creeping silently up the hall toward her door. If only—

Yes, of course, the phone!

She picks it up, dials Peter's number. Peter will come right over, she'll be safe with Peter.

But Peter does not answer the phone.

Where can he be? He must be home, he *must* answer!

But he does not.

She is alone—

The detective! Yes, he said to call. She scrambles in her handbag, finds his number, dials it, drops his card as he answers the phone.

"Yes? Hello?"

She has forgotten his name! The card has fluttered away under the bed. A sudden flash of hysteria hits as she realizes she cannot ask for help to save her life without the social conventions, she doesn't know what to say—

"Hello!" He is angry.

"This is Katie—" she blurts out.

"Are you all right?" He is immediately anxious. He remembers her, then.

"Yes. That is, no. I mean—"

"He called you?"

"Yes. He said he's coming here to get me—"

"Lock your door and windows. Check *all* the windows. Don't open up for *anyone*. I'll be right there."

"Yes, I already have—" But he has hung up.

She walks around the apartment, checking the locks. It is all right now, she tells herself. The detective—what the *hell* is his name?—is on the way. The United States Cavalry to the rescue! She giggles.

She must control herself. She must not give way like this. If only she had someone to talk to, if only she weren't alone. She dials Peter's number again, and again there is no answer. Just when she needs him—

There is no one else she can call at this time of the night without explaining the whole story, and that is too much, too difficult to contemplate doing.

Madame Szilardi.

No, it's the middle of the night. She couldn't.

There is a creak in the hallway outside her door.

One creak, and then silence.

A shiver wracks her, leaving her legs weak and near collapse.

She stands still, listening.

Silence.

Not one sound . . .

She steps quietly nearer the door. Finally she stands right next to it, her ear against it. Listening.

Hearing the deadly silence.

Is he on the other side of the door, listening for her?

Are their ears separated by only one inch of wood?

She strains to hear.

She hears nothing.

But she had heard that creak! Was it only the sound of the building?

Unable to resist the irresistible temptation, she slides back one of the three bolts on the door.

"Don't open up for anyone . . ."

But she is clever. She is not opening the door. She has slid back only one bolt. If he is there, he will have heard it. He won't know that there are three bolts. Will he now try to open the door? Hypnotized, she stares at the handle, waiting for it to start to turn—

Nothing.

She slips back the second bolt.

Does he know there are three bolts? Why doesn't he try to open the door? How could he know?

He knows everything! He has told her so.

Is he there?

She would almost welcome him. Anything would be better than this torture. Anything!

"Don't open up for anyone . . ."

She cannot resist the terrible force of the silence. She slides back the last bolt and throws the door open wide—

The hall is empty.

My God, what has she done? She slams the door shut again and throws each bolt shut. What got into her? What if he had been there, really been there waiting as she opened the door—?

The building is old. It creaks at night—

She is going crazy! She must talk to someone. She dials Peter again.

Oh God. She hangs up again.

She dials Madame Szilardi.

"Hello? Katie?"

"Yes, it's me, how did you know?"

"Oh, my dear, I'm so glad you called. I've just been sitting here for the past hour, I've had the most terrible *feelings*. Are you all right? But of course you're not. What is it?"

She felt better now, just hearing another voice. It brought her back from the world of her imaginings to reality. And if reality included a maniac stalking her, it was still less terrible than the horrors of the mind unleashed at night.

"He called again," she said apologetically. "I'm sorry to bother you—"

"Don't be silly, my dear. I knew he had. And was it worse than usual?"

"Well, he said he's coming . . . to get me."

"You must call the police—"

"I did. Someone's on his way now."

"Good. I'll come too."

"No, it's the middle of the night."

"Well then, I'll come to see you first thing in the morning."

"I'll be all right—"

"Of course, but we'll have a good talk. That always helps. Are you sure the police are on the way?"

"Yes. He said just a few minutes. I'm fine, really. I feel much better now."

"Of course you do. Now go make yourself a nice cup of tea, and if he's not there in fifteen minutes call me right back, and at any rate I'll see you in the morning."

She was a funny old thing, but she was right. A nice cup of tea. Anything to keep moving, to keep busy, to make noise herself so that she would not hear the noises outside in the hall, so that she would not panic again and throw the door wide open to him.

A nice cup of tea, and soon the detective would be here. *What* was his name?

The tea was boiled and steeping in the pot when he knocked.

"Who's there?"

"Gilford."

Was that his name?

"Who?"

"Wally Gilford."

She *thought* she recognized his voice.

"I'm sorry, but how do I know—"

"My phone number is 864-2721."

Yes, that must be him. Still, what if . . . No, she had to trust somebody. She opened the door, and nearly fainted with relief. She actually staggered.

He reached out to catch her. "Are you all right?"

"Yes, I'm sorry. I suppose it's nerves."

"I wouldn't be surprised. May I come in?"

"Of course."

"He didn't show?"

"No. He won't, will he? He was just trying to scare me. I'm sorry I woke you for nothing—"

"Stop apologizing. You think I'd feel better if your throat had been cut when I got here?"

She went pale. She was even more scared than she looked. He cursed himself. And he cursed her; the woman who didn't like cops, he reminded himself. Except at three o'clock in the morning.

He walked around the flat, checking windows. He looked out each in turn, checking the street.

"Would you like some tea?"

He nodded. "Try to remember exactly what he said." He took one last look out the window: there was no one there, the streets were cold and empty.

The street is cold, but not empty.
The beast is out there.
Across the street, half a block down, in the dark phone booth on the corner. He watches the lights go on as Katie dashes from room to room, checking the locks, and he watches as Wally comes running up and enters the building.

And now he withdraws from Peter's mind. Delicately, judging his withdrawal to a nicety, not losing control, in full and firm command he recedes just enough to let Peter look out. He wants Peter to see the man she prefers to him, the man she calls when she is in trouble.

Peter stands there in the dark phone booth, his mind disjointed, not making the proper connections. He is angry at her for being scared. She should know, he thinks, that he would never harm her. He loves her.

He forgets that she doesn't know the calls are from him. He becomes terribly angry as he thinks of her calling this other man for help, ignoring *him*. He doesn't even realize that he isn't at home, that this phone isn't his phone, that she doesn't know where he is.

His mind has split off, as it has done periodically during these last five years. He is forming in his mind an alternative universe, a disjointed and unconnected one, and in this universe Katie has just proved that she does not love him, that she is leaving him, that he is losing her forever, that he will be alone, alone, alone.

Enough, says the beast.
Take me home.

"He's not coming, is he?"

"No."

"It's nearly five. Nearly time to get up."

Wally nods. "Why don't you get some sleep? I'll wait around."

"You must be tired too. Wouldn't you like to go home? I'm not afraid anymore, really I'm not."

"I'll stay for a while."

She looks at him, bites her lip. "You think he *will* come."

"Look, lady, I don't think he *will* come, I don't think he *won't* come, I just plain don't know." Why was he getting angry? "I don't know if he's out there waiting for me to leave or if he's asleep in a warm bed or if he exists at all."

"What do you mean?"

He turns away from her, looks again out the window.

"What do you mean?" she insists.

He shrugs.

"You think I made it all up? Is that what you think? Why would I do that?"

"Why would he call you?"

"He's crazy!"

He turns away from the window and looks directly at her. "Somebody's crazy," he says.

"Me? You think *I'm* crazy?"

He stares at her. Why is he so angry? He doesn't understand it. Why is he involved at all? He never gets involved personally, that's always a mistake. What does he care if this woman doesn't like cops—except, of course, at three in the morning when some nut calls her and scares the crap out of her, then of course she forgets she doesn't like cops. Christ.

"Look, lady, I'm just a dumb cop, right? What do I know about anything except beating up kids and shooting college students and hustling blacks, right? You're the one trying to turn me into an expert: Do I think he'll come, do I think he won't come? I don't know, okay? So you go in and get some sleep, I'll wait around awhile."

"I don't require your services, thank you. I'm sorry I bothered you."

He suddenly laughs. She really looks funny when she gets angry. "Look," he says, "I'm on early shift today. By the time I get home now, it'll be time to go to work. So I'll just stay here."

She shrugs and turns and goes into her bedroom, leaving the door slightly ajar.

What the hell got into him? he asks himself. He must be tired. He wrenches his mind back to the problem. He looks around the room. He wanders quietly around the apartment. He is trying to *feel* the room, feel the aura, get a feel for what is happening here.

He can sense nothing out of the ordinary. Finally he listens at her door; he can hear her breathing deeply. Asleep. He lights a cigarette, slumps wearily in the chair. He should go home now, but he'll wait just a bit longer, to be sure. In the meantime, to stay awake he watches television, keeping the sound low.

Not low enough.

In the next room Katie stirs, turns, suddenly sits up, confused from the sleep, not sure if she's dreaming, shaking with terror. She screams.

Wally runs for her door.

Katie jumps out of bed. She is two steps closer to the door and reaches it first by a fraction of a second.

She slams it shut in his face.

He kicks it open and charges in with his gun in his hand.

Katie has fallen back into the corner. She cringes there, staring at him. "It's you," she says.

"What?"

"It's you! You're the one who calls me on the phone. I heard you!"

He relaxes, smiles, puts his gun away "You were having a nightmare—"

"No! I *heard* you."

They are both quiet for a moment. A commercial from the television seeps into the room. "That's what you heard," he says.

She is confused. "But it was the same voice . . . ."

"Half television, half dreaming," he tells her. He helps her up from the floor and back into bed, when suddenly she says, "There he is!"

She tears out of his grasp and runs into the other room. The commercial is over, the movie has come on again. It is *Witness for the Prosecution*, and Charles Laughton is haranguing the judge.

"That's him," Katie says weakly. "That's the voice."

It is just past seven when Madame Szilardi comes to the door. Katie is asleep; Wally has not turned on the TV again, but is sitting in the easy chair, staring out the window, wondering what has happened to him. He hears a single soft knock on the door.

She knocks softly, thinking that she doesn't want to wake Katie after such a terrible night. If Katie doesn't answer, then she'll just pop off around the corner to a small luncheonette and have a bite for breakfast and try again in half an hour.

Wally hears the soft, single knock and is immediately on his feet. He takes the gun out of his holster. Wally tells himself he isn't scared. If it is the obscene caller at the door, he expects Katie to be alone. All the advantage is his. He tells himself this, but every time in his life he has touched his gun he has always been scared.

He walks quietly to the door. Waits, listening. Then he slides back the bolts, one by one, with his left hand; the right hand hangs limply at his side, holding the gun. He opens the door.

The old woman stares at him.

Then she screams.

Then everything happens very quickly. He lifts his hands in a gesture of appeasement and she sees the gun and her eyes go wider and she screams louder and Katie comes flying out into the hallway and tries to explain, but the old lady keeps screaming, "Call the police! Call the police!"

Wally puts the gun away and tries to calm her down, tries to lead her into the apartment. But as he touches her she fights him off and he tries to stop her screaming and she kicks him hard on the right shin and he instinctively nearly hits her and she kicks him again, this time on the left shin, and Katie begins to laugh.

Wally backs away from the old lady's sharp pointed shoes, and she backs away from him as far as she can get, her back against the wall. They face each other, each unsure what to do next, and in the silence—as she stops screaming for a moment to draw breath to scream again—they both hear Katie laughing.

They turn and look at her. She is leaning against the wall, laughing so hard she can't stand. She can't stop. Looking at the old woman, she points to Wally and tries to say, "He's—he's—"

"He's the one! I can *feel* it!" Madame Szilardi screams, and Katie flies off into another paroxysm of laughter. Which at least puzzles Madame Szilardi sufficiently to stop her screaming. She stands her ground and looks at Wally.

"We'd better go inside," he says.

Katie, subsiding now into giggles, takes Madame Szilardi by the arm and leads her inside. As Wally shuts the door behind them he glances down the hallway; not one of the other doors has opened, no one has heard anything. That old lady's screaming would have wakened the dead, but not the inhabitants of this city.

In the apartment he finds the old lady facing him squarely, arm outstretched, finger pointing. "Katherine," she says, her voice quivering with emotion, "there is great danger in that man."

He turns to Katie, but she is no help at all, still fighting to control the giggles.

"I sense a terrible danger," the batty old woman says, "in his aura. I can almost *smell* it. Katherine, call the police immediately."

Wally takes out his wallet, holds the gold shield out to her. She pauses, takes one tentative step forward, leans forward and squints at it. "Oh," she says, more quietly.

"Detective Sergeant Wallace Gilford, New York Police Department," Wally introduces himself.

"So pleased to meet you. I am Madame Szilardi." She tries to smile. "I'm terribly sorry. You must think me an awful fool."

What could he say?

"I'm so confused," she goes on. "I could have sworn—I can sense these things, you see, and your aura positively *reeks* of danger. Oh, but of course." She was regaining her composure. "You're a police-man. Hence the danger which surrounds you." She turns to Katie. "I was quite right after all."

Katie manages not to giggle, but Wally can't quite suppress a snort. Madame Szilardi turns to him haughtily. "It is an art, you know," she says icily. "Not a science."

PART FOUR

THE BEAST
AT EVEN

CHAPTER

1

Katie sat alone during her lunch hour in the stacks at the library, skimming through psychology books. The stacks, a labyrinth of book-lined caverns which hold most of the volumes in the library, fill the guts of the huge building from top to bottom. Access to them is forbidden to the public, but even so they are a buzzing hive of activity during the day as call slips listing the books requested by patrons are whisked by pneumatic tube from the request desks in the public sectors to deep in the stack innards, where dozens of staff members collect them and plunge through the book-crowded narrow corridors to fetch the books and send them out to the light of day by dumbwaiter. To add to the seeming confusion, the library uses a cataloging system all its own, shelving the books not by author nor by subject but, incredible as it may seem, by size. This system is necessitated by the need to make the greatest possible use of the

impossibly crowded space in the stacks. So all during
the day the caverns are filled with noise and people
and whizzing pneumatic tubes and clanking dumb-
waiters, as messages are sent in and the staff run from
the large books to the small books to the oversize
books and send them clattering out to the people
waiting in the reading rooms.

The library is, in these deepest depths of what is
after all its soul, the very antithesis of its public
conception; there is little quiet, calm, and peace here.
At night, of course, it is a different story. At night the
stacks are empty, deserted, dark and very nearly
haunted.

But now it was Katie's lunch hour and she sat at one
of the few empty tables in the stacks and concentrated
on what she was reading. The disadvantage of the
library's cataloging system is that you cannot go to,
for example, the psychology section and there find all
you want; instead one book on the subject may be on
the first floor east and another on the fifth floor west.
So it would take all her lunch time if she tried to
collect a number of books and take them out to a more
comfortable spot to read. She had become accustomed
to simply looking for a clear spot in the stacks
wherever she found each book and reading it there.

She sat now at a very small table surrounded,
hemmed in, by tall sheer cliffs of heavy books towering over her. She felt perfectly comfortable and at
home.

She was wandering patiently through all the books
on psychology she could find that might tell her
something about her maniac. The detective had been
perfectly honest about the chances of finding him by
normal police work; she was going to give it a try

herself. The key was to understand him.

What did she know about him? Only that he knew her. The voice was false, and so her first guess that he was old could be wrong. But certainly he knew her. How?

Either personally, or through the library, or simply because he had seen her on the TV show. She had thought that he might be the killer she had announced she was tracking, but that didn't make sense. Such a man might kill her, but not frighten her like this. He would have attacked quickly, silently, without warning. Besides, her description had been so vague that no one would have thought it applied to him.

Or perhaps, she thought suddenly, so vague that *anyone* might think it applied?

There are, after all, many undetected murders; there must be thousands of them. Some psychopath she never heard of might be—

No. That opens up too many possibilities. It doesn't bear thinking of. Her job now is not to uncover limitless depths, but to try to narrow down the realm of practical steps she might take.

So then. The calls started a few weeks ago, immediately after the TV program. Possibly coincidence; assume for the moment not. Presumably her TV appearance sparked it off. But why? Here the path she was following branched out again and again, each branch dividing infinitely further until all the trails wound away and were lost in the forest.

She had to know more. She had to learn something of what was going on in his mind. And so here she sat, reading through what descriptions she could find of the kind of mental aberrations that might lead to such behavior.

The possibilities were limitless, bewildering. At first. Then she began to think: she knew a little bit about him. She wasn't working quite totally in the dark. He talked about loving her as well as killing her—and when he talked about fucking her, was that in his mind a combination of the two? He was gentle sometimes, cruel and vicious others, as if he were two distinct personalities. Loving her and hating her, gentle and cruel, two disparate personalities struggling—she went back to her books. She would so love it if she could only show up that snotty detective.

She stopped for a moment, thinking about him. He was so mean; but then so sweet, the way he had run to her quickly in the middle of the night. It was her fault, she supposed, coming on so strongly about all the evils of the police when they had first met. But she had *tried* to be nice since then—God, he made her angry!

She wondered about the innate schizophrenia of all people, about the duality of love and hate. Not that she either loved or hated him of course, but still it was interesting. She wondered what he really felt about her. And then she wondered about the meaning of the word *really*. Did it have a meaning, did it *really*?

Oh no. That way lies madness. She shook off these thoughts and bent again to her reading. She had a wonderful facility for concentration and was soon immersed again, oblivious to the sporadic motion of the messenger staff moving back and forth past her as they fetched and carried.

Oblivious to it all, until suddenly two hands from behind descended on her shoulders, slid down across her breasts and wrapped around her body; a face nestled into her neck, pressing against her throat. Without moving, holding her helpless, a voice came muffled from where his lips were buried, "Guess who?"

Life.

He was getting a firmer grip on life. He was no longer banished to that lost country from whose bourne no traveler ever returns—well, *hardly* ever returns; he was no longer trapped for years at a time, nor even now for months or even weeks at a time. He came out now almost constantly, almost at will.

Not quite. Sometimes Peter put up a fight, but more often these last few days he simply closed his eyes and went to sleep, too exhausted from the constant struggle of too many years now to do battle or even to acknowledge his opponent. It was so much easier to sleep.

And a new development was perhaps even better. He was able now, sometimes, to come out without taking over. He was able to peer over Peter's shoulder, to see what was going on; it was as if he were a leprechaun, one of the wee people, riding about unseen on the shoulder of this great country lout.

The thought struck him as funny; merrily he laughed.

"That's a frightening thing to do!"

"What?"

The girl at the desk smiled up at him. "Coming up to a girl like that and laughing in her face. I might have thought all kinds of horrible things."

"Ah, Suzie, my old girl, like what?"

"Like maybe my lipstick was on crooked—"

"Oh ho, to be sure, and what should a bonny lass like yourself be wearing of lipstick for?" he asked in an Irish brogue so thick it slopped over onto the wooden floor. "With your lips the color of me old mum's heart, and warmer and fuller of life at that. And would you not be agreeable to placing those lips fit for the Mother of God Herself on my own, and to suck forth my immortal soul? Come, sweet Suzan, make me immortal with a kiss."

She laughed. Peter was the most wonderful guy. But why *had* he laughed at her?

"I don't know," he said, settling down. "I didn't realize that I had. I can't remember what I was thinking about, your beauty must have dazzled me—"

"Now don't start up with your blarney again. Besides, I always know what you're thinking about: Miss Katherine McGregor Townsend."

"Ah, sure and begorrah, but it takes a great stroke of hard work for a man to be thinking about any woman, and the likes of you at hand."

"Go on with you now." She tried to imitate his Irish, but somehow it came out faintly Russo-Bulgarian. "Now that's enough of the old blarney."

"'Tis sad indeed I am to see you'll not be falling into bed with me then. Ah well, if that's the way of it, I'll be after asking you the whereabouts of herself."

"She's on lunch break. She's gone off into the stacks somewhere."

"I'll be after searching her out, then, won't I?" And he slipped past her desk with one last smile and walked off into the corridors of heavy books.

Charm, Suzie thought as he went off. Absolutely dripping with goddamn charm. Two more minutes and she *would* be falling into bed with him. Why the hell can't any of *my* boyfriends be actors, she thought. Not that I'd want to marry one, she reminded herself, but still . . .

Still got it, he thought. Still able to put the old double whammy on any lass younger than thirty-five or older than sixty. Wouldn't dare try in the middle range, of course. Nasty they are, the middle-aged, suspicious and envious. They envy Katie's being smart enough to be a librarian and at the same time pretty enough to be an actress; they are suspicious of all the pretty things in life. Including me, of course, he admitted.

Still, as long as he kept out of their way he was all right. Getting back here in the stacks, for example. *Verboten, ganz verboten.* Little Suzie would get a swift boot in the fanny if anyone had seen. But as long as he was careful to approach only the young—who were charmed—or the old—who saw through him but liked the recklessness of youth—he was able to get back here to find old Katie.

And so with the beast perched unseen on his shoulder he wandered through the book-lined caverns from one floor to the other until he found her. At the sight of her, coming upon her from behind, at the sight of her bending so studiously over a heavy tome, totally immersed, his heart warmed and his beast of burden chilled.

There was no one else in sight.

Frighten her, the beast said. Torment her, it commanded.

She's so cute, he said to himself. I love her so.

Kill her!

Play with her. . .

And so he came up silently behind her, placed his hands suddenly on her shoulders, slid them down caressingly across her breasts and wrapped them around her body; holding her tight, he bent over and plunged his lips to her throat and asked, "Guess who?"

She jumped as his hands touched her, but now as he

nuzzled her neck she sat quietly.

"Guess who?" he commanded again.

"I'm thinking," she replied. "Oh dear, I give up, who is it?"

He lifted his head and stared at her. Was she joking? Were there that many men who came up behind her and slid their hands gently over her breasts—?

She was laughing at him. He could see her laughing but couldn't hear her. He could hear nothing but a voice in his ear whispering, "Kill her! Kill the bitch, kill her now!"

He stared at her. There was the sound of footsteps all around them, but nobody was here. They were alone in this corridor.

He could see her laughing, he could hear the voice of the beast, he could sense the world standing still—

He shook his head, shook it violently. And the voice was gone.

"You should see your face." She was laughing. "You look like the wrath of God. Turned the tables on you, didn't I?"

"You knew all the time who it was, did you?"

"Of course. How many men do you think there are who come up behind me and throw their hands around my breasts?"

She was laughing honestly, amused at the obvious jealousy on his face and without the slightest taint of guile—but of course she was an actress.

"I thought you might think it was your new detective boyfriend."

"My what? How do you know about him?"

"He came to see me this morning," he said, pulling over a pile of books and sitting down beside her.

"I hope you didn't mind. I had to tell him about you."

"Of course not. What I minded was that you called *him* last night, not me."

"But I *did* call you. You weren't home!"

"I was home. I was home and alone all night."

She caught at something in his voice—he had been home *and alone* all night—and she realized that she hadn't spent the night with him for a long time. How long? It must be weeks. Why? Had anything happened? She didn't think so, certainly nothing had happened as far as *she* was concerned. It was *his* doing, he had been remote recently—

"I *did* call you," she insisted.

He shook his head. "You didn't," he said, "but I believe you think you did, so it's all right. You must have dialed wrong."

"I suppose I might have," she admitted. "I was shaking with fright." We haven't slept together, she thought, since that damned TV program. She wished she had never done it; it had certainly screwed up her life. No wonder he was remote, he was still hurt by the way she had talked that morning, of her insisting on giving up acting and all that it entailed. It *didn't* entail giving up him, but he found that hard to believe. She could understand that, but she had been so concerned with this idiot who was scaring her that she hadn't been giving any thought to poor Peter's problems. "I did call you," she said more gently. "I really did. You were the first person I thought of."

She hasn't denied that the detective is her new boyfriend, he thought. He smiled at her, and felt sad and lonely.

And the beast sat quietly and watched.

Wally sat, thinking of Katie, talking to himself. I must be a misogynist, he said, that's all there is to it.

How else can you explain my reaction to her? She hates cops, right, but if a guy said that to me in a bar I wouldn't get so mad. Hell, lots of guys have said that to me in lots of bars, and I laugh at them, don't I?

So why am I so mad at her? I guess I'm just a natural-born misogynist.

She's not repulsive, after all. She's goddamned good-looking.

He slammed his hand down on the desk.

Nicely-Nicely looked up.

"Nothing's wrong," Wally said before he could say anything.

"So who said?" Nicely-Nicely asked.

"I'm going for a walk."

"So go."

"I'm going!" He pushed his hat on his head and opened the door.

"Take your coat. It's cold out," Nicely-Nicely called.

He slammed the door.

Thank God he understood himself. Right now, for example, furious at Nicely-Nicely for behaving like a Jewish mother, he understood that he wasn't really angry with Nicely-Nicely. He was angry at that damned librarian.

He took a deep breath. It was cold. He went back inside to the squad room. Nicely-Nicely nodded to him in sympathy as he came in. "Cold out without a coat, right?" Wally felt an instant sympathy for all those who strangle their fellow man. They are driven to it, he realized, by forces beyond their control.

He had always known that, of course, but as a tautology, not as a mental picture of such immediate clarity. He thought of the man who had strangled the girl in Howard Johnson's: What had possessed him?

They had been in bed together, they had been relaxed and friendly, and then—what had happened? Had she made some stupid goddamned comment, as Nicely-Nicely had just done? Or had it been something internal, something originating deep inside the man? Something bursting to get out violently, passionately, suddenly, taking him without warning.

Would he ever know?

Would Marsha marry John? Would the evil forces of capitalist totalitarianism triumph over the peace-loving people's democracies? Would the Miami Dolphins ever win seventeen straight again?

Who knows? Who knows what evil lurks . . .

"What?" Nicely-Nicely looked up from the report he was typing.

"I said, Who knows what evil lurks in the minds of men?"

"The police commissioner," Nicely-Nicely said decisively. "That's his job."

"What's our job?"

"Typing reports." He went back to his typing. He looked up again. "How come you ain't typing any reports?"

"I am a detective."

"Oh, like wow."

"Indeed. At the moment, you may be interested to know, I am working on an intriguing case involving desperate desperadoes and an evil genius intent on working his nefarious ways on an innocent maiden. Not maiden in the sense of virgin, you understand."

"Maiden in the sense of made in every hotel room in Manhattan, maybe?"

"Not exactly, although your alliteration does you proud. As a matter of fact, she's an old friend of yours."

"Yeah? Who?"'

"Remember the broad who called you a couple of nights ago, the one with the phantom caller?"

"Yeah. So what?"

"So she's a TV personality of sorts, and the captain wants her body protected."

"So how come he didn't give it to me?"

"You want it, you can have it. I don't want it."

"I don't mean that, what the hell would I do with it? I just meant, you know, why not me? I took the squeal, right?"

"And brushed her off, right?"

"Hell yes. Wouldn't you?"

"Hell yes," Wally agreed. "Nothing personal. You just weren't around when our valiant captain had the bee put in his bonnet."

Nicely-Nicely was satisfied. That was all right then. "So what's it all about?"

"I don't know. Probably nothing. But there's a boyfriend . . ."

"Ah-*hah!* *Cherchez la femme*, right? You talk to him yet?"

"Yes," Wally said. "I talked to him this morning."

"So what do you think?"

"What's it matter what I think? I'm just a dumb cop."

"So are we all," Nicely-Nicely agreed, and went back to his typing as Wally went back to his thoughts of the boyfriend.

Peter.

The actor.

By the time Madame Szilardi had stopped screaming this morning at Katie's apartment it had been too late for anyone to go back to sleep, so Katie had dressed and made coffee and they had all sat around the kitchen table and discussed the situation. And Wally had zeroed in on the boyfriend, on Peter.

"Tell me about this guy," he had said.

"Who?"

"This Peter."

"He's not a *this Peter*, he's just Peter. My friend."

"Friend? Lover?"

Katie glanced at Madame Szilardi.

"Don't bother about me," that lady said. "I know the way of the world, I shan't be shocked."

Still, her ears pricked up slightly and her nostrils twitched when Katie said, "All right, he's my lover. It's nothing serious, though."

"It isn't?"

So there it was, lying out there in the open, staring her in the face. *Was* it serious? The cop was sitting there, not sipping his coffee, just looking at her with his cop's eyes—*Just give me the facts, ma'am*—and she had to decide.

"No," she said. "We're friends and lovers, but it's not serious."

"What's he do for a living?"

"He's a waiter at the Café du Mille."

Wally's eyebrows lifted. "I thought the waiters there were all French?"

She laughed. "You should hear Peter's accent."

When Wally looked a bit puzzled, she said, "Oh, of course you don't know. He works at the restaurant between jobs, but really Peter's an actor. A very good one." And she went on to tell him about everything, about how she was no longer an actress and Peter was bothered by that because he was so dedicated.

And all the time Wally was thinking, the man is an actor, the man can do accents.

The voice on the telephone is Charles Laughton,

and the girl's boyfriend is an actor. If there are four voices any actor can do, they're Cary Grant, James Cagney, Humphrey Bogart.

And Charles Laughton.

Which of course proves nothing. If half the nuts in the world think they're Napoleon, there must be at least a decent percentage who think they're Charles Laughton. In fact, half the nuts who *do* think they're Napoleon probably think that Napoleon talks like Charles Laughton.

So it proved nothing. Nevertheless, there was no doubt in Wally's mind when he left Katie's apartment just exactly where he was going.

He walked down the block to Broadway and turned down past Zabar's. The address she had given him turned out to be a brownstone on Seventy-fourth Street with garbage cans out front and six black men sitting on the front steps and ten million potted plants in the first-floor windows and inside a dark hallway and stairs leading up, up, up. The kind of building, he thought, that's been getting more dirty and disgusting every year for the past fifty years and soon it'll be bad enough that somebody'll buy it and kick everyone out and paint the place and sell it for $2.8 million.

He found Peter still asleep in a small flat on the fifth floor. They faced each other in the open doorway, Peter trying to wake up and figure out who this guy was who had woken him and was flashing a gold Woolworth's badge in his face, Wally trying to identify himself and get his breath back at the same time, not to mention hoping the calf muscles in his legs wouldn't cramp from his climb into the stratosphere.

"You want to come in?" Peter asked.

"That would be nice."

Wally sat down in a soft chair and Peter put on some coffee. By the time it was ready, Wally's heart had stopped racing and Peter had rejoined the living. As he poured the coffee, Wally told him about Katie's calls last night.

Peter was upset. "Why didn't she call me?" he asked.

"She did. No answer."

"I was home," Peter said. "I was right here."

"That's what I was wondering about. Where could you have been at three o'clock in the morning?"

"Right here."

"Up late last night?"

"Not particularly. Why do you ask?"

Wally looked at his wristwatch. "It's nearly twelve. I obviously woke you up."

Peter shrugged. "Sometimes I sleep a lot. I can hit twenty hours at a stretch. Occasionally."

"Maybe that's it, then."

"What?"

"Last night. Maybe you were so sound asleep you didn't hear the phone ring."

Peter shook his head. "I heard you knock, didn't I? I would have heard her. She didn't call."

"She says she did."

"What do you want me to tell you? I was right here all night. I was asleep, but I never sleep through a ringing phone."

"So she must have dialed the wrong number."

Peter shrugged. "Must have. Does it matter?"

"I'm just trying to understand what happened."

Which was true, of course, but sufficient unto the day is the necessity thereof and what he was really trying to do was empty his mind and let Peter's reactions filter in and then try to get a *sense* of what Peter was all about.

He couldn't do it.

He sighed and took out his notebook. "Okay," he said, "just for the record, tell me all about yourself."

So Peter told him about being an actor in this demi-paradise, he told him about the jobs he had had in this city and about the jobs he had had in other cities: Atlanta, Hyannis, Louisville, they're not the Big Apple but there's a whole world out there in rep. On the other hand, what the hell, if you're going to make it you have to make it right here in New York. And Wally listened and wrote down what he thought might be significant, dates and places, and he knew all the time they weren't significant, nothing is significant, what's the point? Finally he left the apartment and walked aimlessly down Broadway, trying to get a handle on Peter and failing.

And he knew why.

What he had to do was empty his mind and then play like on a videotape everything Peter had said, the way he had reacted to each question; he had to look at that mental videotape and then analyze it, looking for anything false in Peter's reactions. And then he had to decide why it was false. Was it from nervousness, guilt, fear?

But he couldn't do it.

He couldn't look at the videotape with a blank mind, he couldn't analyze it unemotionally. He was getting too much static from his own feelings.

He *wanted* Peter to be guilty.

Christ.

Ridiculous.

Why would he want that? What did he care?

The more he thought about it, the angrier he got. He

knew when he was talking to that damned woman that he was getting involved and he knew that was wrong. He couldn't clear his mind, he couldn't clear away his feelings. He shouldn't be angry at her, he shouldn't have any feelings at all for her, he shouldn't be *involved*.

Start from scratch. Cold and clear. At the beginning.

Girl appears on television, tells the world she tracks down murderers, is on the track of one now.

Girl gets obscene calls. Calls turn threatening. From her murderer?

Possible. Not likely.

Most crimes, at least most violent crimes, involve family or lovers. Do we have anything like that here?

Peter.

Peter is an actor, he can do accents well enough to work as a French waiter.

So was he lying, this Peter? When Wally told him about the phone call last night, was that the first he had heard about it? His reactions were troubled, upset; that was natural. Was it innocent? Did Peter really know nothing about the phone calls?

Wally stopped in his tracks, breathing in the cold December air, standing stock still on Broadway and Sixty-second Street, bumped by the people who filed around him and stared at him as if he were crazy: another Broadway nut, so what else is new?

And he sighed.

Yes, he decided, Peter is innocent.

He really did know nothing about the calls.

Proof?

He shrugged, and began walking back to the precinct, hands in his pockets. He was a detective; he *knew*.

And don't start shouting at me about getting involved, he told himself sternly. It's reasonable that I'd want the boyfriend to be guilty; he's all I've got. If it's not him it could be anyone in the world, anyone from Mr. Hyde to Jack the Ripper. That's the only reason I wanted old Peter to be guilty.

And when something inside himself wanted to argue that point, he wouldn't answer.

CHAPTER

2

He was wrong, of course, but he was also right. Peter *did* know nothing about the phone calls. It is the beast making those calls, not Peter.

Peter knows, of course, that something is wrong. He feels a restlessness inside him, he feels a vague longing, a dissatisfaction, a tremor of fear. He wonders sometimes who he is. And don't we all?

He is no more aware that part of his soul has split off and formed a malignant growth than others of us are aware that some of our liver cells or stomach cells or skin cells are beginning to do the same. And as the cancer grows unseen and unfelt in our bodies, multiplying and dividing irrationally, taking over the body and killing it almost before its presence is suspected, so Peter's cancerous soul is growing unseen, becoming more powerful each day, each night.

And so that day, when Wally left him, the beast whispered in his ear that something was obviously

going on between that detective and Katie. Was he the
reason she was quitting show business?

Nonsense. They had just met.

Of course. But *if* they had just met, why had she
called him instead of you when she was frightened in
the middle of the night?

She did call me.

Did she?

She said she did.

He said she said she did.

Why *wouldn't* she call me?

Why *didn't* she call you?

She did!

The phone . . . did . . . not . . . ring . . .

I didn't hear it!

You *would* have heard it. If it had rung.

She dialed the wrong number.

Or she dialed the right number. . . . *His* number . . .

I don't know. I don't know . . .

Of course you don't. Find out.

How?

Talk to her. Go see her. And if she lies to you—

She won't lie. Katie never lies to me.

If she lies to you—

Katie loves me!

If she lies to you . . . kill her.

And so Peter went to the library to find Katie, to
talk to her about last night. That was when he found
her in the stacks and crept up behind her and wrapped
his arms around her body and whispered into her ear,
"Guess who?"

"I did call you," she said gently. "I really did. Yo
were the first person I thought of."

Peter smiled at her. He believed that she thought

she had dialed his number, but he also noted that in their conversation she had never denied that the detective was her new boyfriend.

He felt sad and lonely.

He smiled at her, sadly.

She smiled back, brightly. "I'm going to stay here late tonight," she said. "I'm going to read every book they have here on psychology and I'm going to work out who this maniac is—"

"You're a real nut," he said.

"What?"

He gestured at the pin she was wearing on her sweater.

She looked down at it.

"I LOVE NY," it said.

She smiled. "Why am I a nut?"

"You've got this creep scaring you out of your mind and the cops say they can't do anything about it, how can you love this city?"

"I do, though. That's exactly why I wore the button today. I got up and was dressing and saw it on the bureau and I thought I *do* love this city. No damned maniac's going to take this city away from me. I'm not going to take my phone off the hook or get an unlisted number or run away and hide. This is *my* city, and if he thinks he can scare me out of it he can go fuck himself!"

Peter had to smile. He lifted his hands and clapped. "Bravo," he said. "This sceptered isle, this earth of majesty, this other Eden, demi-paradise, this little world, this precious stone set in the silver sea, this blessèd plot, this earth, this borough, this Manhattan hath made a shameful conquest of itself. Hath it not?"

"Mayhap it hath," she said, "but it's my home sweet home. Anyhow—"

"Anyhow?"

"Anyhow, I'm going to come back here tonight after closing and work all this out. But I'm going to have to break for dinner. Can we meet?"

Katie frequently works late at the library. Sometimes as part of her job on those nights when the library stays open till nine, sometimes as part of her hobby when she goes back there at night for her "research." Frequently on such nights she meets Peter for an early supper at the café; the restaurant opens at five, but there are very few customers before six and both Peter and Katie are favorites of the *patron*, who allows Peter to share a rear table with her and who frequently joins them himself.

Peter shakes his head. "Busy tonight," he says. "Can't make it."

"What's up?"

He looks away. The conversation has taken a wrong turn. *He* is supposed to be interrogating *her*. In fact, he quit the Café du Mille two days ago and he doesn't want to tell her. Why not? Well, why should he? Is it any of her business?

He is defensive about it because, in fact, he himself doesn't know why he quit. The beast hasn't told him. But three days ago he simply slept through his appointed time at the restaurant. The next day again he didn't show up. When his friend the *patron* called to find out what was wrong, he quit.

He doesn't know why. He doesn't want to think about it, he certainly doesn't want to talk about it. "I've got an audition tonight," he says.

That's unusual enough for Katie to ask, "Where? With whom?"

"With *whom*?" he mimics angrily. "*Whom* the hell do you think you are? I *know* it's correct, only nobody on this goddamn earth talks like that except *you*, do you know that?"

"I'm sorry," she offers, surprised, astonished at his outburst.

"Never mind. *I'm* sorry. Who am I to tell you how to talk?"

"You're—"

"I *know* who I am. *Whom.* Your quondam lover!"

"Peter—"

Silence.

They look away from each other. Neither knows what to say.

"Sorry," he says. "I'm nervous about this audition."

"You'll do well. You're a good actor."

"Yeah. Sure. It's a new group, one of these outfits that gets a lease on a loft on the East Side and right away they're entrepreneurs. Nothing will come of it."

"Maybe something will."

"Nothing will come of it. But anyhow I can't meet you tonight. Look, I better go off and meditate myself into some kind of shape, right?"

She watches him as he kisses her on the cheek and turns and walks down the narrow aisle of high-piled books, as he waves at the end of the aisle, as he disappears behind the books and is gone.

She wonders why he is so upset. Clearly it is because of her. Somehow it is her fault, but she is not sure just exactly *how* it is her fault.

Peter doesn't know why he told her all that about the audition; the beast hasn't told him yet. He doesn't know why he is so irritable. He doesn't know that he is struggling to keep the beast in; he doesn't know that he is struggling and losing.

He has no audition, he has no job, he has nowhere to go. But he doesn't leave the library, he doesn't leave the stacks. The beast whispers in his ear, and he wanders around the miles of corridors, seemingly aimlessly.

Only *seemingly* aimlessy. The beast has a very definite aim. He is looking for something. And so he directs Peter down to the basement, where they find a corridor Peter has never noticed before. It ends in a door, which opens to another corridor, which again bends and turns and ends in yet another door.

This door has a sign on it: *Emergency Exit Only, Alarm Will Sound If Opened*. There are wires along its edge, leading to what must be the alarm. He reaches up and pulls them loose.

He waits, nothing happens.

He opens the door.

The alarm does not ring.

He looks out through the door. It leads into a small courtyard, and beyond that is the park bounded by the library on the east, Forty-second Street on the north, Sixth Avenue on the west, Fortieth Street on the south. It is surrounded by an iron fence.

He closes the door, tucks the wires up so they are out of sight. The door locks automatically when it closes. He opens it easily from the inside, but as he looks at the outside of it he sees that there is no way to open it from out there once it is closed.

He goes back down the hall, around the corner and through the other door. He finds the circulation room. He asks the librarian in attendance there for some Scotch tape. She is happy to help him. He tears off a six-inch long strip and thanks her.

He goes back to the emergency exit. He opens it and tapes the catch shut, the way he saw the Watergate burglars do in *All the President's Men.*

Now the door can be opened easily from the outside. It can be opened and the alarm will not ring. Now he can leave the library and come back whenever he wants.

Unless, of course, the security guards here will be as conscientious as the one that caught the Watergate burglars. He smiles. He doesn't think that's likely. Probably no one has tried to break into the library for a hundred years or more.

Not that *he* wants to break into the library . . .

He frowns. Why *did* he rip the wires loose, tape the door open?

He doesn't know.

He doesn't *want* to know.

He is terribly tired. He wants to go home.

He wants to sleep.

But why did he tape the door open?

Never mind, his head hurts, aches terribly, a blinding migraine, oh Christ, he just has to get home, he has to go to sleep before his head bursts—

Blindly, he leaves the library, stumbles down the wide stone steps, turns up Fifth Avenue. He forgets everything, he wants only to get to the safety of his own home.

CHAPTER

3

"So, Wally, what do you think?"

Wally shrugged. "I'm just a dumb—"

"Yeah, I know. You're just a dumb cop." Captain Moller sat at his desk, looking at Wally. "Twenty years you been saying that. Twenty years you been the smartest cop in Manhattan and you been sitting on your ass saying that instead of taking the goddamn lieutenant's exam. Sometimes I wonder about you, Wally."

Wally wondered if that's what they taught you when you became a captain, or if that was just the sort of thing people who become captains automatically know: When you want to appear particularly sincere and friendly and concerned, use the first name. Fifty weeks of the year he was Gilford to the captain, but twice a year he became Wally. He wondered if the captain even realized he was making the switch.

"Well look," the captain was saying, "when they start paying me to be a psychologist instead of just a dumb captain, maybe then I'll worry about dumb cops who are too goddamn dumb to take an exam they could pass easy because they're so goddamn smart. In the meantime, you're the smartest dumb cop I got so I'm asking what do you think?"

"I don't know—"

"Don't give me any of that smart-ass stuff, okay?"

"I mean it, I just don't know. She's not faking it, I'm sure of that."

"Okay, that's something. How are you sure of that?"

"That's a stupid question and you know it. How is anyone ever sure? You talk to the broad, you see her reaction, if after twenty years you don't know if someone's faking it or not you're in the wrong business. Am I right?"

"You're right. So she's not faking it. I just thought, a spinster librarian, you know, maybe she's looking for a little attention."

Wally laughed. "You haven't seen this spinster librarian. All she has to do is walk across the room and everybody in the damned library is watching those hips. Believe me, she's not looking for attention."

"So the calls are for real?"

"They're for real."

"So who is it?"

"That's what I don't know. There's a boyfriend, but I don't think it's him. So it could be anybody."

"Someone who saw her on TV?"

"Almost certainly. The calls started right after the program."

"I don't like it. With my crummy luck this broad's

gonna get her fucking throat cut. You got anything to go on?"

Wally shook his head.

"It could be anyone out there," Captain Moller said despondently.

"I guess so, if you think it's possible that there exists a nut or someone of a criminal bent out there among the ten million law-abiding citizens of Our Town."

"Okay, I guess you can find something else to keep you busy."

"You taking me off it?"

Captain Moller looked surprised. "You just said there's nothing you can do, right?"

"And you just said with your lousy luck she's going to get her fucking throat cut, right?"

"But if there's nothing you can do, there ain't much you can do. I mean, am I right? Am I misunderstanding the situation? So go do something you *can* do. There's ten new calls on your desk since yesterday."

Wally shrugged. He stood up. He walked to the door. "She's not gonna get her fucking throat cut, Captain."

"No? How come?"

"The guy on the phone keeps talking about strangling her."

"You're a great comfort, Gilford, you know that? You ever think about becoming a priest?"

"Hey, what do they call a beautiful girl in Poland?" Nicely-Nicely asked.

"I give up. What?"

"A visitor."

Wally stood just inside the door, hands in his pockets, lost in thought.

"Hey, get it? A *visitor*. A beautiful girl in Poland."

"Oh. Yeah. That's really very funny."

"Well look, you win a few, you lose a few. What are you gonna do, shoot me for trying? So what did *mein Kapitan* say?"

"He took me off the librarian squeal."

"Great, 'cause we got a rash of burglaries on Amsterdam—"

"Amsterdam? There's nothing left to burglarize on Amsterdam. What are they stealing, the rats?"

"Hey, that's good, that's very good. That's almost as good as the Polish visitor. You think maybe Amsterdam jokes will replace Polish jokes? How do you stop five black kids from raping a white girl on Amsterdam?"

Wally stared at him.

"Throw them a basketball," Nicely-Nicely said. "Get it?"

Wally stared at him.

"You don't get it," Nicely-Nicely sighed. "Never mind. So what it looks like is it's a gang of kids and they just move through a whole building like the goddamn seven-year locusts. So what we're gonna have to do is pick a spot and stake it out and wait for them."

Wally stared at him, not seeing him.

"So I could really use a little help on this, okay? You hear what I'm saying to you? The captain says I can have two uniforms but you know how much help they're gonna be, I could really use you, too, you know what I mean? Okay?"

Wally picked up his hat. "I think I better talk to her one more time," he said.

"Who?"

Wally stared at him.

"Sure." Nicely-Nicely shrugged. "Who else? So listen, give your librarian my love."

"She's not *my* librarian."

"Sure. And listen, put on your coat," he called as Wally disappeared through the door. "It's cold out there! It's December, for Christ's sake," he muttered, turning back to his typewriter.

He stepped out onto Fifty-fourth Street and turned right toward Eighth, but first he had to step off the sidewalk and into the street to walk past the precinct building because the pavement was obstructed with piles of uncollected bags of garbage.

On the corner of Eighth Avenue there was another obstruction. As he approached, he could see the flow of pedestrians coming up against an impediment, curling around it in a kind of human turbulence, and then flowing on again down the avenue.

He felt a momentary temptation to curl around the perimeter himself and continue on his way, but instead he pushed through to the center. You never know what you're going to find in the center of things in this city.

What he found was a middle-aged, very squat and fat black woman with a bandanna around her head and a long skirt reaching to the ground and a large suitcase and an overflowing straw-handled basket at her feet. She was standing right in the flow of pedestrian traffic. The hurrying people came bumping right up against her before parting and flowing to either side and hurrying on. She turned from one face to another, trying to ask something, but before she could get the words out that person was gone and she was bumped by the next.

Wally stood on the upstream side of her, breaking the flow of traffic, his feet clamped firmly to the sidewalk against the bumping and pushing, not giving an inch. He bent down to her. "Can I help you?"

At first he couldn't understand a word she said, but finally one word came through clearly: "Nigeria."

"Nigeria?" he asked.

She smiled for the first time and nodded her head excitedly. "Nigeria, Nigeria!" She pointed to herself and then spread her arms wide.

He nodded and picked up her heavy suitcase and the straw-handled bag and stepped into the street. She followed quickly behind him, waddling like a fat duck. He stopped a cab cruising up Eighth, opened the door and put her inside, handing her bags in after her.

"Where to?" the cabbie asked.

Ignoring him, Wally stuck his head inside the cab and asked if she had any money. She stared at him uncomprehendingly. "Money," he repeated. He took out his wallet and held it open to her. She nodded excitedly and dove into her large bag.

"Hey, Mac, where to? I ain't got all day," the cabbie insisted.

She pulled a smaller bag out of the large bag, opened it, and held it out to Wally. He reached inside and took out a handful of money. Nigerian money.

"Beautiful," he said.

She looked worried.

He smiled at her.

"Look, buddy, we're stopping traffic. We're creating a disturbance, you know what I mean? I could get a ticket!"

Wally handed the woman her money and closed the taxi door. He turned to the driver's open window. He took a deep breath and counted to three before answering; it's bad for the digestive system to lose your temper on an empty stomach. "How much will it be to take her to Nigerian Airways?"

"To where?"

"Nigerian Airways."

"Where the hell's Nigerian Airways?"

"I don't know where it is. *I'm* not driving a cab in this city!"

"Jesus fucking Christ, there're ten million goddamn fucking people in this city, you expect me to know every fucking address? I ain't never been to no Nigerian fucking airline, how the hell should I know where the fuck it is? Now I would very greatly appreciate it if you would take this lady out of my cab and let me go pick up a fare that knows where the fuck he wants to go, would you mind?"

It's a terrible temptation to carry a gun in New York City, Wally thought. Someday I'm going to pull it out and blow the face off somebody.

"Take a right at the corner," he told the cabbie. "Lufthansa's on the corner of Fifth. Go in there and ask them where the Nigerian airline is. If they don't know, tell them to look it up." He took out his wallet. "Here's five bucks. It's probably somewhere with all the other airlines in the next block or two on Fifth. Keep the change."

"What if it ain't?"

"What if it ain't what?"

"What if it ain't right there with all the other airlines? What if it's a six-or seven-dollar fare, what do I do then?"

"Then you don't keep the change," Wally said. "You're taking a gamble."

"Gambling ain't legal in this city, buddy. Why don't

you take the broad and shove her off on some other hackie? Do me a favor, huh? Come on, let's go, out!"

Wally held the five-dollar bill out to him.

"Out!" the cabbie repeated, shaking his head. "Get her outta here! Do I *need* this aggravation?"

Wally flipped open his wallet and showed the gold shield. He took out his pen and notebook. "Name and ID number?" he asked.

"Hey, what the fuck? What did I do? Just said I didn't know where the goddamn airline is! Is that a crime now? Did I say anything else? I'll take the broad, relax."

"I'll take your name and ID number," Wally said, "just in case the broad doesn't get to the Nigerian airline without being raped, robbed, and thrown out into the street."

"Hey!" The cabbie was genuinely angry. "What the hell do I look like?"

"Believe me, you don't want me to tell you," Wally said, and wrote down his name and ID number.

The cab drove off and he walked down Eighth toward Forty-fifth Street. He liked to walk crosstown on Forty-fifth, he liked the theaters and the restaurants and the seedy tone of years gone by. But first he had to walk down Eighth, down past the porno theaters and the porno stores, the *Super Stud* posters and the massage-parlor advertisements handed out as he walked by, and the hookers leaning against the buildings. He had nothing against the concept of sex for sale; sex is a beautiful thing and it ought to be free for everybody but if it isn't, at least it ought to be cheap and with no restrictions. But the *sleaziness* of the porno business was so—Christ, *sleazy*. And the thought of getting into bed with one of those filthy, scabrous, disease-ridden hags who are simply walking *pissoirs* for the dregs of quote humanity unquote—the thought was enough to make him nauseated.

He turned up Forty-fifth with relief. Between Sixth and Seventh avenues a young black kid shambled up to him and asked him for a dollar for lunch. All the old arguments rose up: Why couldn't the kid get a job, *any* job, there must be better ways of getting money than begging for it. But the kid was shaking and skinny and sick and Wally reached into his pocket for his wallet. As he brought it out he was bumped from behind and the skinny sick little kid grabbed the wallet out of his hand like lightning and took a quick step into a sprint away.

More quickly, Wally hooked his foot around the kid's flying ankle and sent him sprawling. He whirled and caught the other one, a burly black man, with a chop into the throat. As he gagged, Wally dove on the kid, yanked his hair back by the braids and planted his foot firmly in the small of his back. "One move and I yank and break your neck," he told him.

He took out his gun and turned to the other one who, choking, had taken a step toward him and was reaching out to grab him. "Freeze," Wally said. "What's the expression? Motherfucker? Freeze, motherfucker, or I blow your brains out."

The man froze.

Wally let the kid up. He looked around. The street was suddenly deserted. He marched the two in front of him up the street. He put his gun in his jacket pocket with his hand on it; he didn't want to attract any more attention than was necessary.

At the corner of Sixth he found a cop. He told him that these two had tried to snatch his wallet and that he wanted them arrested.

"No, you don't," the cop said.

"I don't?"

"Nah. If you insist, I have to arrest them. But then you know what happens? I gotta book them."

"That's the idea," Wally said.

"Nah, that's not the idea," the cop insisted. "I book them and then you get an order for a court appearance and you have to take off from work to show up, but *they* don't. 'Cause they been released on cognizance and why should they show up? So we reschedule it and maybe we find them and so then you get another court appearance and you come back again and if they show up this time they got a lawyer who's paid for by the city and he gets them a continuance 'cause he ain't had time to study the case properly and then you're gonna get another letter for another court appearance, and you know you're gonna miss five or maybe six days from work and whata' you gonna get out of it? Even if they get convicted they're gonna walk right out on probation 'cause there ain't no place to put them. So it's gonna cost you more time than it's gonna cost them, believe me."

Wally took out his wallet and showed the patrolman the gold badge. The cop shrugged. "You're the boss," he said. "But you know the story as good as me. Why don't you just take them up some alley and beat the crap out of them?"

"What can I tell you?" Wally asked. "Run them in."

He walked down Fifth Avenue. On the north side of Forty-second he passed a bag lady leaning over, reaching halfway inside an overflowing can of trash, searching deep down on the bottom with her outstretched, dirty fingertips for the necessities of her life.

It was as if she were invisible. No one else seemed to see her. The traffic light was red and people stood waiting all around her, looking up in the air, looking at the traffic light, looking right through her. Nobody saw her.

Maybe they're all tourists, Wally thought. Maybe they're all from Ohio and they've got their own troubles back home. I *can't* be the only one in this city who gives a damn. There's ten million people in this city; some of them *have* to care.

The light changed and he crossed the street and walked up the wide stone steps into the library. He asked for Katie and found her in the Berg Collection. He walked through the empty room and up to the desk and she looked up at him and smiled brightly through her reading glasses and he saw the button on her blouse.

I LOVE NY.

He couldn't help it, he had to laugh. "You and me, kid," he said. "We're both crazy."

Dinner.

Restaurant La Rousse, on Forty-second Street west of Tenth. Katie had suggested the restaurant. It was Wally's first visit, and after they had ordered he sat back and looked around and said it was very nice.

"Wait till you taste the food," Katie said. "And the prices aren't bad, are they?"

"Everything seems lovely," Wally agreed. "Except, just maybe, the walk here."

Katie nodded. They had walked straight down Forty-second from the library. "I usually walk down Fortieth," she said.

"Naturally. Only an idiot would walk down Forty-second."

"Then why did you insist we come that way?"

He shrugged. "It's the shortest route," he said. He looked at her. "And because I wanted you to see it. I wanted to ask you how you can wear that button if you know that Forty-second Street exists?"

"It's not pretty," she agreed. "I know we have a problem—"

He laughed. "A problem? That reminds me of the captain of the *Lusitania* whose last quoted remark was, 'I think I heard a noise.' That's no problem out there, that's a terminal disease. It's not an isolated sore spot, it's spread all through the city. We're drowning in these people. Hell, they're not even people, they're animals!"

"What can we do?"

"Get rid of them!"

"How?"

Wally didn't answer.

"How?" she repeated.

He shrugged. "For one thing, when they're convicted of crimes, send them away. Put them in jail. Only there aren't enough jails to hold them all. So we have to raise taxes to build jails. But we can't raise taxes because the people scream; they'd rather be mugged than taxed."

"They wouldn't *rather* be mugged, it's just that no one thinks the mugging's going to happen to him, but they know the taxes will."

Wally shook his head angrily. "They *kill* people, and they're back out on the street before we finish typing up the paper work. It's ridiculous."

"But what's the solution?"

"The death penalty, for one thing. Not a death penalty on the books that gets applied once every five years and then it takes ten years of appeals before anything happens and it costs the state over a million dollars, which we could have used to build new jails— I mean a real death penalty, so if somebody kills somebody, *wham*, he's executed."

"I *knew* you were going to say that," she said indignantly.

"And I knew what your reaction was going to be," he snapped. "They should be rehabilitated, right? They should be made useful members of society. Don't you people understand by now that it can't be done? They are not human beings—"

"I am not *you people*," she flared. "I am *me*. And," she continued, "if you're going to call me a bleeding heart, I am going to throw this glass of water in your face!"

He stopped suddenly, subsided, even laughed. "Actually, I was going to call you a do-gooder."

She looked at him, took her hand away from the glass of water, and laughed with him. "This is where I came in, isn't it? The bleeding heart pinko do-gooders against the fascist pigs."

He nodded. "We're laughing," he said, "because we see how silly it is for two grown people to fall back on name calling like a couple of angry kids. But the reason we're so angry is that we know we have a devastating problem and we don't know what to do about it. I used to believe all that crap about rehabilitating the criminal classes, but it just hasn't worked. We've tried it. They come out of the jails and the halfway houses and the detention centers worse than they went in. Even the mental hospitals haven't been any good. For instance last year, maybe you read about it, in the Village some guy tried to kill his wife, he just all of a sudden went crazy—which I know is silly, people don't all of a sudden go crazy. They slowly develop neuroses which become transformed into psychoses and all that stuff, or maybe it's a chemical imbalance, but okay I'm no psychologist so he went crazy all of a sudden and tried to kill his wife. The cops got there and stopped it, caught him, he went to trial, and he's innocent by reason of diminished responsibility—"

"But that's all right! There's nothing wrong with that, they're not going to turn him loose on the streets, they give him treatment, they try to *cure* him—"

"Right. Beautiful. They try to cure him. The operative word there is *try*. What happened is he's committed to the state mental hospital, after six months he's beginning to make progress—he's not cured, you understand—but he's beginning to *relate* to the outside world in a constructive fashion, and the doctors give him the weekend off so he can begin to adjust to the outside world and he leaves the hospital at ten o'clock on Saturday morning and he goes home and kills his wife."

"Oh God."

"Right. He went home and slit her throat and sat there and waited for us to come get him. Now wouldn't it have been better if that poor nut had just been executed right off the bat? Better for society, better for his wife, better for his parents and her parents, and better for his own immortal soul, whatever the hell that may be. Wouldn't it have been better all around?"

She didn't answer. Finally she said, "That's only one example."

"Are there any others where the poor nut was cured

and returned home to lead a normal life? Does that *ever* happen? Look, take this nut that's calling you. You probably think of him as a poor, sick man who needs to be cured."

She nodded.

"Okay," he said. "Up to a point I go along with you. If we've got some poor little guy sitting alone in his room and trying to make contact with the world out there in this pathetic way, trying to feel like a man by coming on strong with the pretty librarian, I agree he's just a neurotic little twerp and maybe a doctor can help him. But if it gets worse than that, if he actually crawls out of his hole and puts his fingers around your throat and tries to murder you, then it's gone too far, he's beyond the point of being cured. He's a horse with a broken leg. It's a shame, it's a tragedy, it's a waste of the precious human potential, but they shoot horses, don't they? He's got to be killed. Otherwise they'll just put him away for a few years and when he comes out he'll kill again!"

"Not necessarily—"

"Right! Not *necessarily*, but look, if there's a hundred people like that, my solution is to kill the hundred. Your solution is to put them in the hospital. If you put them in the hospital, maybe you'll cure ten of them, but then the ninety others come out and if they each kill one innocent victim, have you really been a success? Is that progress? I've got a hundred homicidal maniacs dead, you've got ninety innocent people dead, which way is the world better off? And don't tell me the cure rate for psychopaths is greater than ten percent, it's actually pretty goddamn close to absolute zero!"

Instinctively she reached out and put her hand on

his. "Can't we talk about this without your getting so upset?"

"Katie," he whispered hoarsely, "I'm *drowning* out there! You sit in that library and the only people you see are good people, people who read books. The only time you know about this other world is when you walk down Forty-second or some nut calls you in the middle of the night to tell you he's going to kill you! But I live with these people every day and every night, I'm swamped with them. Right now I'm not supposed to be sitting with you, did you know that? My captain took me off your case. He said leave her alone, we don't have time, let her get murdered."

"He didn't!"

"He did! Not in those words, but that's what he means. He doesn't *want* you murdered, but he knows that the odds are that this guy is never going to show up, and while I'm sitting here taking care of you there are literally thousands of crimes happening in this city and there aren't enough cops to cover them, to write up the paper work, let alone get around to solving them or helping the victims. We're drowning in rapes and muggings and murders—"

"Then why are you here?" she asked.

Well, that was the big question, wasn't it? That was the question Wally had carefully avoided asking himself ever since he had stalked out of the precinct house and across town to the library.

He shrugged, not looking at her, but she wouldn't take that for an answer. "Why are you here?" she insisted. "You're a detective sergeant, didn't you say? If a captain takes a sergeant off a case, then he's off it, isn't he?"

Wally looked at his watch, then looked up and tried

a smile. "It's after six," he said. "I'm off duty."

"Then you should be home, shouldn't you? Won't your wife mind when you don't show up for dinner?"

"Why do you assume I'm married?"

"I'm not assuming, I know you're married."

"How could you know that?"

She seemed momentarily just a bit flustered. "Well, you know," she said, "I told you I'd been back in the stacks, trying to understand something about the psychology of my nut, or *maniac*, as you call him, and do you know the way books are arranged in the stacks? They're not by subject matter but by size, so that according to subject matter they're all jumbled around and, well, while I was looking for a psych book I just happened to come across a yearbook, I think it's called, from the police academy and I just happened to glance through it and it was the year you graduated and there you were. Wallace Gilford, born in Queens, 1935, graduated from CCNY, 1956, married, 1957."

He nodded.

"So I ask again," she went on more confidently, "if your captain isn't angry for your having dinner with me on police time, won't your wife be angry for your having dinner with me on her time?"

"She won't mind," he said. "She's dead."

"Oh. Oh, I'm sorry. It never occurred to me—"

"It's all right. It was a long time ago." He took a deep breath and looked at the high ceiling. "She was killed ten years ago."

"I'm sorry. I didn't know."

"It doesn't matter now," he said.

She looked at him and saw that it mattered very much now. Instinctively she said the right thing. "Tell me about it."

He had never talked about it. Cops are tough and strong, cops see people killed every day, cops don't talk about it. Not even when it's their wife. No one had ever said, "Tell me about it."

Quietly, he told her. About the murder, the loss, the pain. About forgetting her face in the night, about never forgetting *her*. Quietly, finally, after ten long years, he talked it out.

He told her about the '66 Chevy, about his quest. "That's why I've never taken the lieutenant's exam," he explained.

"Why not?"

"They take you off the street."

"What does that mean?"

"When a detective becomes a lieutenant, the first thing that happens is they take you off the streets. You're too important to keep on doing what you were doing as a sergeant and you're not senior enough to command a squad, so they put you behind a desk. You're now a detective of proven intelligence, you've passed a test, so instead of letting you solve crimes they put you in charge of arranging the work detail for, say, Manhattan South. Or they put you in charge of logistics or operations or liaison or laundry or toilet paper. Then after a few years of that, maybe when somebody dies, they let you take his place in charge of a squad and you're a real detective again. It's like putting in your time in purgatory before they let you back into hell."

"But that's the only avenue of promotion, so what choice do you have?"

"All the choice in the world. I don't have to take the damned exam. If I don't take it, there's no way they can promote me out of sergeantry, there's no way they can take me off the street. And I want to stay on the street because I want to find that car and those hoods that killed Peggy."

There was a long silence, and then Katie said softly, "You're not going to find that car now, you know. It was almost certainly stolen to begin with, and now, ten years later—"

"I know. I know. But there *was* a chance. Even if it wasn't much of a chance, it was the only chance I had. The storekeeper was dead and Peggy was the only other witness, and she was dead too. The only chance was either find the car or catch them in a similar crime. And the only way I could do either of those was to stay on the street."

"But you're not going to catch them now, are you? Not after all this time?"

"No. But you know how it is, after a while things become a habit. There's no one point at which the chance of finding that car drops to zero, it just slowly gets less and less and all of a sudden the years have gone by and you don't even realize it. And what the hell, I wouldn't want a desk job anyway, so I think I'll just stay a sergeant the rest of my days."

"Because of your wife?"

"Her name was Peggy."

"Because of Peggy?"

"Yes."

Katie took a roll out of the basket and began to pick at it. Looking at the roll, she said, "Do you think she would have wanted that?"

"She doesn't want anything," he said brutally. "She's dead. The only thing that counts is what I want."

Katie shook her head. "It can't be what you want. You're not happy," she told him.

"Happy?" The question had never occurred to him. "Happy?" he repeated. He sounded tough again.

Katie kept picking at the roll with her fingers. She gave just a quick glance up and saw that he was staring off to one side. She could see the pain in the drawn lines of his face. He didn't look like a tough cop. She didn't know what to say. Finally she took a chance, and again her instincts or her empathy or her feelings or *something* led her to choose the right words. "Why did you come to the library tonight to see me?" she asked, changing the subject.

He looked back at her. The pain disappeared from his face, wiped out by the impact of a vague embarrassment. "I don't know," he mumbled. "There were some questions I wanted to ask you."

"Questions?"

"Well, you know. What we've been talking about."

"But all that doesn't have anything to do with the case, does it?"

"I guess not."

"You're not really worried about my telephone caller, are you? You don't really think he'll try anything."

"I guess not," Wally admitted.

"You just wanted to see me again," she insisted.

He shrugged.

"You did, didn't you?" She wouldn't let him off the hook.

"I guess so."

"But it was I who suggested dinner. You came to see me at the library and I told you I was going off duty but that I was coming back this evening after a quick dinner and all you said was 'Oh.' So I suggested you join me for dinner, didn't I?"

He nodded.

"If I hadn't, you wouldn't have asked me, would you? You would have just gone away again."

He shrugged.

She stared at him in amazement. "You're shy, aren't you? My God, a shy cop!"

"Here's the soup," he said with great relief as he saw the waiter approach like a Saint Bernard, saving his life.

As they ate the soup their behavior was sufficiently bizarre to elicit amused comment from the several couples sitting around them, who noticed that at first—when the soup was served—the man lowered his eyes to it and immediately dove in. The girl ignored her soup at first, sitting instead with her elbows on the table and her chin on her hands, staring at him. Under the force of that look he finally glanced up, and when he did she immediately looked down toward her own soup, picked up her spoon, and began to eat. Whereupon he lost interest in his own soup and stared at her, and then she would look up and he would look down and the whole process would reverse itself again and again until all the soup was gone.

"What are your plans for tonight?" he asked.

"Back to the library," she said, wiping the last drop of soup from her lips. "I'm determined to try to understand that nut, and there are still a lot of books to go through."

He looked at his watch. "It's after seven already. Doesn't it close at nine?"

"Yes, and we're not supposed to stay there after hours, but there won't be any problem as long as I get in before nine. The security guards are friends of mine. I can stay as long as I like."

"I don't like it. You'll be all alone there "

"You said you weren't worried."

"I'm not. I'm sure this guy isn't going to try anything. But it doesn't hurt to stay on the safe side. I mean, in a city like this anything can happen. And being all by yourself in an empty building—"

"But it's not empty," she laughed. "I told you, there are security guards all over the place."

"There may be security guards there, but they're not all over the place. Believe me, I know how these operations work. They're there to keep away the casual prowler, but no one is really worried about tight security at a place like the library. So you'll be sitting at a desk someplace and there's got to be a good thirty minutes to an hour in between the guards' rounds. You'll be completely alone for those stretches of time. It's just not a good idea."

"I admit it's kind of a creepy place when there's no one else there," she said, "like being all alone in an old castle. But it's really the safest place in the world. All the doors are locked and the windows are barred. No one can get in."

"He could hide in the men's room at closing time and be waiting for you when you come back." He could see the sudden shock of fear as he said this, and quickly he reached across the table to take her hand. "I'm sorry," he said, "that was a stupid thing to say, I didn't mean to scare you. But I *am* a little worried."

For a second she left her hand in his, then pulled it away and laughed. "No need at all to worry. He couldn't do that because nobody knows I'm going to stay there after closing except you. He couldn't lie in wait for me if he doesn't know I'm coming back, could he?"

He nodded. "Right," he said. "The brilliant big-city

detective strikes out again."

They studied each other until the waiter came and placed the main course before them. They finished the meal without much conversation, each of them going over his or her own thoughts. They had filtre coffee and passed up dessert; then they stood and put on their coats and hats and left the warm restaurant and stood for a moment on the sidewalk, breathing in the cold fresh night air. Then they started up Forty-second Street toward Tenth Avenue.

"You know," Wally said, "I didn't not ask you out because I was shy. I mean, it's just that I've never asked anyone out since—you know. I've never wanted to. I don't know, maybe I am shy or something, because I did want to see you but I didn't know what to say."

"I understand," she said, and took his hand.

They walked a few steps, and he said, "For example, I mean about going out with girls. The only experience I've had in ten years was with the Widow Kellerman."

"The Widow Who?"

He told her about the widow. They began to laugh. "It's not easy," she said. "The swingles scene in New York City."

And they walked up the street laughing. And he thought, they were right. They were right after all. You do finally get over the pain. Like a headache that finally fades away. It just takes longer than everybody said.

At the corner of Forty-second and Eighth they stopped.

"I live up that way," he said, pointing up the avenue.

She nodded. "I work up that way," she said, pointing up the street.

He nodded. "Well look," he said, "I'll call you tomorrow?"

"That would be nice."

"Right." He paused. "The thing is, be careful tonight."

She smiled. "Don't worry."

He nodded. He wasn't worried. Nuts that call people on the phone aren't likely to—

Aren't *really* likely to . . .

He made up his mind and firmly took her by the hand and led her across Eighth Avenue and up Forty-second Street. "I think I'll come back with you," he said, holding her hand tightly. "I'll just check out the men's rooms before closing. That way I'll *know* you're safe behind locked doors."

Locked doors.

Peter closes the refrigerator door, opens it again. It is not locked. Refrigerator doors do not lock. Why is he thinking about locked doors?

He stares into the interior of the refrigerator. He is hungry, it is past dinner time and he has not eaten. Did he eat lunch? He doesn't remember. He had gone to see Katie at the library . . .

He closes the refrigerator door. He is not hungry. He is restless. He will go out.

To where?

He doesn't know. The room is a closed jail. Locked doors. His skin itches, he would like to slip out of it like a snake. But he is caught inside it, locked inside it. He can't get out.

He has felt like this before, he knows the feeling

well. He is getting sleepy. Soon he will fall asleep, and then it will be all right. Going to sleep is like opening the door, when he is asleep he can get out. And then when he awakes again he will be all right. It has happened before.

All he has to do is sleep . . .

No!

He is frightened.

Like being caught in a recurring nightmare. You know it has all happened before . . .

What has happened before? What is so frightening?

He doesn't know. Like a nightmare, it starts out slowly, naturally, nothing to be frightened of . . . except that vaguely he knows what is happening, knows that something frightening is going to happen, knows that he cannot stop the inevitable nightmare . . .

No!

Not this time.

He will not let it happen, he tells himself, not this time, not again, not ever again. He knows he has done something terrible, those other times. He doesn't know what, he doesn't remember anything, but he is aware that he has fallen asleep and has wakened somewhere else and he doesn't remember what has happened but he knows it is something wrong, something bad, something terribly frightening.

Where is Katie? He needs his Katie.

No. Not your Katie. Not anymore.

He spins around to see who is talking. But there is no one there. He could swear he heard a voice, a small voice right next to his ear, as if from someone perched on his shoulder.

But he is alone in the room.

He struggles to stay awake. He begins to pace up and down. He will walk. He knows it has something to do with Katie. He walks up and down . . . his skin itches, it is loathsome, vile, he retches—he has to get out!

If he could only sleep. If he could only close his eyes and relax, if sleep would come . . .

Locked doors.

He must not sleep.

A plan. In desperation, falling before the onslaught of the sleep that swirls in on him, he thinks of a plan. He goes to his front door, turns the key that slides the dead bolt home, securely locking the door from inside as well as out.

Locked doors.

He laughs.

He is locked in now. He can't get out.

He is safe.

Katie is safe.

He takes the key and walks to the window and throws it out. It sails through the air and falls to the street four flights below, clanks and bounces and is lost in the night.

Oh, thank God, now it is safe to sleep.

He can't hurt anyone now. He can't hurt Katie.

His last thought as he falls asleep is how silly that is. Hurt Katie? He would never hurt Katie.

Hurt Katie.

His last thought merges with his first thought as his eyes open again the very next second, as they open bright and clear.

Hurt Katie.

He laughs.

How silly Peter is after all, how stupid! Did he think locked doors could keep him locked in here? Any more than they could keep him locked out of the library? Absurd.

He sits up quickly in bed.

He stands up, ignores the hallway to the locked front door, crosses instead to the bedroom window.

He opens the window and climbs through it, four flights up. He steps onto the metal slats of the fire escape.

Quickly he climbs down to the street and disappears into the dark.

As Katie and Wally entered the main entrance hall of the library, the girl at the reception desk called them over. "You had a phone call, Katie," she said. "I told her you weren't on duty tonight, but she said you'd be back."

Katie looked at Wally. "But nobody knew I was coming back tonight."

"She said she knew you'd be here," the girl said, "and to ask you to please call her. Madame Szilardi. Here's the number."

"How did she know you'd be here?" Wally asked. "You said no one knew."

"I can't imagine," Katie said as she dialed. "Hello, Mada—Cynthia?"

"Katie darling, I'm so glad you called! I knew you'd be there. That twit who answered the phone said you weren't working tonight, but I told her I just *knew* you'd be back. I've been calling your apartment all evening just in case I was wrong, but I wasn't wrong, was I, because there you are! You *are* calling from the library, aren't you?"

"Yes."

"I knew it! Now, my dear, I don't want you to be

frightened, but . . . are you alone?"

"No. Detective Gilford is right here."

Pause.

"I don't trust that man."

Katie laughed. "Don't be silly. He's a policeman."

Madame Szilardi snorted. "I thought *you* were the one who didn't trust policemen."

"I was wrong. I was a pinko commie bleeding-heart do-gooder." She smiled at Wally.

"I don't trust him. I sense danger there. Of course, it's only a feeling . . . ."

"I'm sure he's a good man," Katie insisted.

"Well. I do trust your instincts. And he's right there beside you?"

"We're practically touching."

"And you're not picking up any wicked vibrations?"

"I'm afraid not."

"You trust him?"

"I trust him."

"Well . . ." she sounded skeptical, but then said decisively, "if you say so, that's good enough for me. You don't know it yourself, but you have powerful instincts, I can tell. He must stay with you, then."

"Why?"

"Oh, didn't I tell you? I've had the most alarming premonitions all afternoon. Now you know that's very unusual in the afternoon. Sometimes when one gets them at night they mean nothing at all. Indigestion, you know, which one is prone to at my age. Especially after pastrami. But in the afternoon, when I've had nothing but toast for lunch. And some tea, and just a slice of cheese. Nothing at all, really. Well, you see what I mean."

"I do."

"Then you'll be careful?"

"Very careful."

"Katie, you're not taking this seriously!"

"But I am, I promise you."

"Let me speak to the detective."

Katie handed the phone to Wally with a smile and a shrug. She watched him as he talked to her. "Yes," he said, and then "yes" again, and then quite a long while went by when all he did was nod his head and listen.

She did trust him, she was thinking. Was she getting old, she wondered, to begin trusting policemen? Did this happen to all young radicals in the fullness of time? But she didn't feel old, she felt younger than she had in years . . .

"I promise," Wally said. "I'll take care of her, you don't have to worry. Right. Of course."

Finally he hung up. He and Katie looked at each other and began to laugh.

Peter is standing outside, on the corner of Fifth Avenue and Forty-second Street, looking up at the library. It looks like a mausoleum, he is thinking. It will *be* a mausoleum, he thinks. It will encompass one dead body tonight.

One dead librarian will rest among the books tonight.

But he must wait, wait until the library closes at nine o'clock and the staff leaves. Until Katie is alone.

He wanders down Fifth Avenue, past the lions.

Nine o'clock.

Closing time at the library.

Wally was hanging around the third-floor men's room, getting funny glances from the last of the customers to leave. Finally, when everyone should have been out, he checked it carefully. He stuck his head into each cubicle—

"Looking for something, buddy?"

He spun around. A security guard was standing there watching him. Wally showed him his badge and explained that, quote, they had reason to believe, unquote, someone might be lurking around the premises. The guard promised to keep his eyes open.

Wally walked down the stairs to the main floor. On the left-hand side, behind the large stairway into the main hall, there is a fairly well-hidden cavity almost as large as a room, piled with boxes. Wally slipped over and behind the banister and checked through every box large enough to hide a man. By the time he climbed out, he was satisfied that Katie's nut was not lurking anywhere in the building.

She was waiting for him by the front door.

"Everything all right?" he asked.

She nodded.

If everything was all right, then there was no need for him to stay. The building was locked tight, and it was empty except for the occasional security guard wandering around. She'd be safer here than in her own apartment, he told himself.

Then why did he feel so—

What?

Creepy.

He turned around and looked back at the main hall. The ceiling was more than four stories high, the hall itself larger than most public buildings. The two great staircases along the right and left walls curved up and away into the distance. With most of the lights turned off and the people gone, it resembled nothing so much as an ancient castle.

An ancient haunted castle.

"Spooky," he said.

The walls, the floor, the ceiling, all were made of cold and solid white stone. No wood, no carpeting, no wallpaper, nothing to bring it up into the twentieth century. Cold stone, empty vast rooms—

"I like it," she said. "It's cozy, in a sense."

"Cozy? That ceiling's high enough to have thunderclouds and lightning, and there are enough empty corridors—"

"—to harbor a dozen ghosts," she agreed. "Isn't it delicious? But unfortunately we don't have thunderclouds or lightning or ghosts, there's nothing here but books. Nothing to be afraid of."

Then why was he afraid? Christ, he was getting like—what was her name?—Madame Szilardi. He was *feeling* things. Some cop.

"Right," he said. "I'll give you a call tomorrow."

Nine-fifteen P.M.

Peter wanders around the park behind the library, walks around the block, ambles casually by the library entrance. He knows the place closes at nine, he knows also that it takes time to empty, time for the staff to close the drawers of their desks and gather their papers and their coats and say good-bye and walk down the long corridors and finally leave the building.

Nine-thirty.

Activity has finally ceased. It has been several minutes since the last person left. The building is dark and quiet, although he knows the night security guards are still inside. And so is Katie.

He walks around the corner to where the iron fence surrounds the park behind the library, down Forty-second Street to the gate. He turns into the park. He walks a dozen steps and then suddenly sits down on a bench.

Quiet.

No footsteps.

No one has followed him. He is alone. Unseen.

He gets up and walks down the path to the back of the library building, to the emergency exit. It is quite dark here. He is alone.

He pulls at the emergency door.

It opens easily, quietly.

Inside the only light is a dim hallway bulb.

He slips inside the building and closes the door behind him. He is strong and sure in his movements, confident and alive. If only Peter could see him now, he laughs.

If only Peter could at least remember him when he wakes up!

"I'll give you a call tomorrow?"

"That would be nice."

"Just to check, to see that you're all right."

"Of course."

Wally looked at her, frowning. "Well," he said, and turned toward the door. He was halfway through it when he stopped, hesitated, and came back to her. "You know what I was thinking?"

"I can't imagine."

"You know the way you caught that guy? The guy who murdered his wife, the one you talked about on television?"

"I didn't catch him. I only—"

"Yeah, I know. You found that he had done the same thing before in another town. I was thinking maybe I ought to be doing that."

"Looking for a man who makes obscene phone calls in other cities?"

"No, no, nobody's gonna write a newspaper story about something like that, things like that happen every day. I was thinking about this other case I'm working on, where a girl was strangled in a motel room a couple of weeks ago. It's a very weird case. Maybe if I check the papers for other towns around here, something similar might turn up. You know what I mean?"

She shook her head. "It's not a good idea. For a hobby, it's all right. I can afford to spend my spare time looking up things like that in papers because I enjoy it, but it's not an efficient use of a policeman's time. It took months and months and months before I found what I was looking for in that case. It would be a waste of time for you to do it."

"Not official time. I don't mean that."

"What do you mean?"

"Well, I agree it's not an efficient way of doing things and I couldn't justify to my captain spending all day in the library reading old newspapers. But I was thinking, like, well tonight I've got nothing to do. I'd just as soon sit here and read old newspapers as go home and read an old book."

"What old book are you reading?"

"Trollope. I'm halfway through the Palliser novels."

"Believe me, you'll enjoy the Pallisers better than the papers."

"I think I'll give it a try just the same."

"Wally."

"Yes?"

"I'm really all right here. I'm quite safe."

"Hey, who said you weren't? This has nothing to do

with you, this is another murder entirely I'm working on. Listen, if we cops didn't spend most of our spare time working on cases, we wouldn't even be solving the ten or fifteen percent of the crimes that we do manage to clear in this city. You just set me up with the old newspapers and then you can go about your business, okay?"

Peter is in the stacks.

He knows there are security guards in the library at night, and he knows there are not enough to cover adequately such a large building. There are aisles upon aisles and corridors upon corridors on every floor of the stacks; he could hide there if even a thousand guards were patrolling.

He goes slowly, quietly, ready to duck up another aisle if he should hear a footstep coming down this one.

But he hears nothing. The stacks are quiet and empty.

He makes his way up from the basement.

Wally worked steadily for an hour and then pushed the stack of papers away in disgust. He could spend a year down here and not cover a fraction of the possible towns and cities and nearby counties in which the murder he is seeking might have occurred, if it ever did. And why would it have had to happen nearby? Even a nut can buy an airline ticket.

He leaned back in his chair and wondered if Katie was all right. Perhaps he should check on her.

Perhaps he should get his head examined.

There was a telephone on the desk by the entrance. Katie had promised that if she heard any strange noises she would call him immediately—but there weren't any phones in the stacks. Of course, she could always duck back into the office space and grab a phone . . .

Maybe he should check on her? But how could he? He didn't know where she was. It could take him hours to find her, and if she needed him while he was searching she'd be calling him here and the phone would be ringing and he wouldn't be here to answer it. Shit. He'd better stick to the plan. It was an old axiom in police work: Never change your plan in the middle of an operation. And never, *never* change it if you can't notify your partner of the change.

He turned back to the pile of newspapers.

Impossible. If only he knew where to start.

If the murderer were only Peter . . . . He laughed at himself. It didn't take a Brandeis psych major to figure out where that thought came from.

Still . . . he had started out on this case working on the assumption that the nut calling her might be someone close to her. If it was a total stranger, the chances were that he was getting his rocks off just by calling and there was no further danger. The only chance of danger came if it was somebody closely involved, and the only person he had turned up was Peter. And Peter would be capable of imitating Charles Laughton, he was certain of that.

All of which is hardly proof. It is not even barely suggestive, he told himself sternly, unless you happen to be a cop who is cracking up from too many years chasing too many punks and who has suddenly been faced with a pretty face.

He stopped for a moment to consider that. She certainly had a pretty face.

How many years had it been since he had thought that about anyone?

Never mind, get back to Peter. Even if Peter was the caller, which was not very likely, could he also be the strangler?

But how about the caller's insistence on feeling his fingers around Katie's throat?

He shook his head. He was letting his imagination run away with him. It was that damned Madame Szilardi with her nutty premonitions. But more than that, it was spooky here, late at night, large empty rooms with high resonant ceilings, long dark shadows . . .

Katie was on the third floor of the stacks. She sat at a small table at one end of an aisle of books, a lamp on the table her only light. The narrow aisle, hemmed in by the tall shelves of books, seemed to stretch out into the darkness, out into infinity, out over the edge of the world. On all sides of her, identical aisles stretched out in parallel lines to the darkness where the dragons lay.

She laughed. At the childish scariness of being alone in a vast, dark hall. She laughed out loud, and as the sound of her laughter died away she heard the terrible quiet seeping in from the dark.

What was that?
Peter stops.
Listens.
Nothing.
Nothing, now.
But he had heard it.
Laughter.
A sudden laugh in the quiet stacks.

Katie's laugh.
She is here.
Over there, somewhere, to his right.
Quietly, quietly, he turns.

Impossible.
Impossible to go through all those newspapers.
Wally sat at the desk and grimaced in disgust. What
was he doing here, anyway?

He leaned back in his chair and reached for a
cigarette. He saw the No Smoking sign and put it
away again. He asked himself what he was doing
there, sitting in an empty library pretending to be
trying to find a murderer in the newspapers.

Nonsense. He was here because he was worried
about Katie.

Also nonsense. There was no possible danger unless
the caller was somebody tied very tightly emotionally
to her, and there was no such person except Peter and
there was no proof of any kind—there wasn't even an
indication of any kind—that Peter was mentally
unbalanced. If there had been anything linking Peter
to that motel murder, that would be a different story,
but there was nothing.

One minute. Wait one minute.

When Wally had interviewed him, Peter had listed
his activities for the past few years. He had mentioned
the other towns he had worked in, the theater com-
panies he had worked with.

It was a long shot, of course, but if a cop didn't
follow up on his hunches he had nothing to do but
spend all his days sitting at a desk. It was a
ridiculously long shot, but at least it was better than
trying to sift through every paper published in the
United States.

He checked the dates he had written in his note-book, then got up and went over to where the *Atlanta Journal* was stored.

Katie heard a noise.

Her head shot up from the books, her eyes darted around, her ears nearly prickled. She took off her reading glasses, held them in her hand.

She looked, she listened.

No sound. No movement.

Not in the small circle of light from her desk lamp. But beyond, in the darkness?

There was no one there, of course, there couldn't be anyone there. She had probably heard the echo of the guard's footsteps . . . .

But it was spooky here. Scary.

Nonsense. Scary for a little girl, perhaps. Not for a grown-up librarian.

On the other hand, it wouldn't hurt to take a break. She walked down the aisle to the door leading into the office area, opened it, and walked across the room to the desk in the center. She could call Wally on the internal line, but instead she dialed 9 to get an outside line and call Madame Szilardi. If she called Wally, he'd insist on coming up to her, he'd recognize the tension in her voice. And she wanted only to relax for a moment.

"Hello, Cynthia," she said.

"Darling Katie, are you all right?"

"Perfectly."

"No sensations of danger?"

"None whatever. I'm having a lovely evening, just called to be sure you weren't worried about me."

"But I *am* worried. Is that detective with you?"

"No—"

"Then you're alone! Katie, quickly, go find him!"

"But you don't trust him!"

"I don't, and I do. I trust you, and if *you* feel he's all right I have to believe it. The important thing is that you not be alone tonight. Do you really want me not to worry?"

"Of course I do."

"Then I think I'll come in to stay with you."

"Don't be silly. I'll be finished here and home long before you could get here."

"I suppose you're right."

"Of course I'm right. Now I have to get back to work—"

"Where is he?"

"Who?"

"The detective."

"He's right downstairs, in the newspaper room."

"Are you sure?"

"Of course I'm sure. I can give you the extension down there, you can call him yourself if you don't trust me."

"I didn't mean that—"

"I know, I'm only teasing. But let me give you the extension anyhow, and he'll tell you we're really quite safe in here."

She gave her the number and listened to all the warnings about taking care of herself, and felt immensely cheered up. That was just what she had needed to remind herself how silly her fear was.

Frightened of the dark! Like a child.

Smiling at herself, she got up and left the desk, walked across the empty room, back through the door into the stacks.

Leaving her reading glasses behind, on the desk next to the phone.

* * *

In the quiet of the stacks, Peter had heard her voice on the telephone. Not quite able to zero in on it, he had left the stacks by the door next to hers, had come into the room near her.

He stands there now, by the connecting door, listening as she leaves the room and goes back to the stacks. He waits a moment, then goes into the room Katie has just left.

He wanders around, feeling her presence. He comes to stand by the desk.

He sees her glasses. He recognizes them. She has forgotten them; she will be back.

He looks at the telephone, notes the extension number.

He goes back to the room next door.

Waiting.

Katie comes back into the room, goes straight to the desk, sees her glasses next to the phone, reaches out to pick them up—and jumps in fright as the phone rings.

She stares at it.

Insistently, it rings again.

It must be Wally, she thinks, and picks it up and says, "Hello," and only then realizes that it cannot be Wally; he doesn't know that she is here by this phone. She realizes it only then, and by then it is too late.

"With my fingers around your throat," Charles Laughton says, "you will die tonight."

A spasm of terror—she thrusts the phone away from her, reaches out with it to hang up—and then the sudden realization of safety. For if he is calling her, he is somewhere else. And she is safe in here, locked in here with the world locked outside and Wally waiting downstairs where she can call him at any moment.

With that realization comes a spark of courage, and she asks him, "Why do you talk like that to me?"

"Because he loves you."

"Who loves me?"

"Peter."

"You know Peter's name?"

"Oh, cunning bitch. Ask not for whom the bell tolls. It tolls tonight, my dear, my bitch, it tolls tonight for thee."

Her mind is racing. She is not frightened now, she is thinking too hard to be frightened. He knows Peter! So he is not a stranger—and again there is a chill of fright. For Wally had said that there was no danger if the caller was a stranger, there is danger only if he knows you personally. And he knows Peter, so he *does* know her personally.

But never mind. He is locked out there somewhere. He can't possibly get in. She mustn't waste time being afraid, she must talk to him, she must find out more about him. Who is he? A friend of Peter's? A jealous friend?

"Why should you mind if Peter loves me? Do you love me?"

"Me?" Charles Laughton laughs. "I'm going to kill you."

"Why?"

Pause.

"To punish Peter."

"For what?"

"Does it matter? Do any of these questions matter? Can you think of nothing more interesting to ask about on the night of your death? Are you not interested in the infinities? In the darkness of the cosmos?"

"Do you know about that?"

"I am a creature of the darknesses, I come from the infinities, I am driven by the Furies."

"You have a soul too sensitive to be talking of murder. Why are you so lonely?"

No answer.

That is the key, she thinks. He is lonely, alone, separated from other people by his own psyche. Why? A cripple, perhaps? She tries to think of Peter's friends, of someone who might feel outcast—

Oh my God!

Terror.

Sheer terror, so that her fingers tremble and she nearly drops the phone.

She has noticed the extension light.

The phone is a Centrex model, including four extensions with separate numbers which can be answered at the push of a button. When one of the extensions is being used, that button lights up. Her own button is lit, of course, but so is one other. Which means that someone is talking on that extension.

But the library is closed. There is no one else here.

No, wait, don't panic. *She* is here; perhaps someone else is also working late. Perhaps one of the security guards is calling home, perhaps . . .

"Two souls are one soul," Charles Laughton is saying, "and one soul is sufficient to tighten—"

She pushes the other lit button, switching to that line.

"—fingers around your throat, hold them tight around your throat, watch your face as you gasp for breath—"

He is on that line!

He is on both lines!

But—

The only way he can be on both lines is if he is calling *to* her line *from* that line.

He is inside the library.

She slams down the phone. Her light goes out. In another instant, so does the other light. He has hung up.

He is in this building. He is going to kill her.

She listens.

She hears nothing. A cold, empty, dark, silent building—

There! Was that a sound?

Oh, God. She lifts the receiver again, dials the number of the newspaper room—

The phone rings.

Wally glances up at it. Katie? Is anything wrong? He picks up the phone. "Oh," he says, smiling. "Good evening, Madame Szilardi. Now how did you know where to reach me?"

Busy!

How can the line be busy? Whom can he be talking to? She hangs up, dials again.

Busy!

She slams the phone down. Damn him!

Was that a sound?

Where?

He is somewhere in this building.

Where?

"Something terrible is going to happen!"

"Nothing is going to happen. I promise you."

"How can you promise me?" Madame Szilardi moans. "You won't *do* anything!"

"I'm right here with her—"

"*Where* are you?"

"Right here," Wally says. "I'm sitting right next to the telephone, all she has to do is call if anything bothers her."

"You're sure?"

"Of course. And there's no one in the building except a bunch of security guards. She's perfectly safe—"

"Oh dear!"

"What's wrong?"

"What if she's trying to call you now? Your line will be busy!"

Wally smiles. "Then maybe we'd better hang up."

"Yes, let's do! Be aware!"

"I will. Don't worry."

"Good-bye then."

Wally starts to say good-bye, but she has already hung up. She's a sweet old thing, Wally thinks, but mad as a hatter.

He goes back to the *Atlanta Journal.*

There!

That definitely was a sound.

Katie holds the phone in her hand, about to dial Wally again. She doesn't dare move. She stands quietly, listening—

Yes!

She is sure that was a sound!

She drops the phone and runs to the door into the stacks. He'll never find her in here. There are floors and floors of aisles and corridors here, there must be hundreds of miles of narrow passageways lined with old, heavy books, dark and narrow and offering refuge.

She runs blindly up one of the aisles.

The room she has left is empty. For a moment.
Then the connecting door to the next room opens,
and Peter comes in. He stands there quietly, listening.
Dimly, he hears the sound of her running footsteps.
He opens the door to the stacks and walks quietly
up the aisle after her.

In his notebook Wally had jotted down the places
and dates of Peter's out-of-town work. Of course, Peter
might have lied, but that would have been silly; for an
actor, it would be too easy to check.
And indeed he finds now in the *Atlanta Journal* an
advertisement of the show Peter had worked in. So all
he has to do is work his way through the five weeks
that Peter spent in Atlanta last year.
On the thirty-fifth day he finds it.
The last day of Peter's sojourn there, a murder in a
motel, a strangling, identical to the Howard Johnson's
murder two weeks ago.
He can't believe it. Seldom a hunch turns out right.
It could still be just coincidence. He has to check
other cities, other dates.
The next on his list is Hyannis, Massachusetts, two
summers ago. Hyannis, that's Cape Cod. What paper
covers Hyannis? He turns to the index, finds nothing
under Hyannis; but under the C's he finds the *Cape
Cod Times*.
If Peter is the Howard Johnson's murderer then he is
also Katie's caller; he must be, otherwise the coincidence is too strong to believe. And if he is, then the
caller is not a poor sick little harmless nut, he is a
psychopathic murderer. Not only potentially dan-

gerous, but a psycho who has killed and killed again.

Where is Katie?

He looks at his watch. It is over an hour since he left her.

He looks at the phone.

Why hasn't she called?

Because she's busy. Working away in the stacks.

Where in the stacks?

If he searches for her, he leaves the phone unattended.

Wait. First find out whether the Atlanta murder was coincidental. Check out Hyannis. Nothing to worry about right now. Peter doesn't know she's here tonight. The library is locked.

Give Katie another half hour. If there was a murder in Hyannis and if she hasn't called in, then he'll look for a security guard and search for her.

No reason to worry yet.

Katie runs blindly into the stacks, up this aisle, down that one, until finally she realizes she is racing around like a madwoman, with no sense of direction or destination. She collapses onto the floor, sits there trying to gather her wits and her breath.

It will be difficult for him to find her here, but also difficult for Katie to escape. There are no phones, so how can she summon help? Wally is her only hope; how can she reach him?

She hears footsteps.

He is in the stacks. He knows she is here.

She gets to her feet, edges away. If he sees her—

Her hand brushes the light switch on the wall. She flips it off; the floor is plunged into darkness.

Scary. But safe.

She knows her way around here better than he does. Perhaps she can make her way to the exit before he finds the switch.

Death in Hyannis Motel.

A quiet, two-point headline on page six, not to alarm the tourists.

The date is July 31, 1979. Closing night of *Streetcar.* Peter's last night in Hyannis.

An unidentified young girl, quietly strangled in her sleep. No motive known, no suspect arrested.

Wally looks at the phone. It remains silent.

He checks his watch. No reason for her to call, no reason to be worried.

But he is worried.

He leaves the newspaper room, looking for a security guard. The halls are empty.

You can never find a cop when you want one.

He climbs the stairs to the next floor.

"Katie?"

She shivers in terror.

It is Charles Laughton calling her, in the pitch-black stacks.

"Katie, my dear, my bitch. Naughty child. I'll find you, you know. Eventually, before morning, before anyone comes for you, I will find you . . . ."

She realizes he is trying to make her panic. Trying to make her run, so that he might hear her, because he cannot see her, cannot find her in the dark. She must remain still. The darkness is her friend. But if she simply sits here, sooner or later he *must* find her.

She edges her way along the stack of books, nine feet high. She feels along the stacks with her hands. Slowly—she must not stumble.

She comes to the end of an aisle. She reaches out blindly with her hands. She feels nothing. What if he is out there? What if she is reaching out to his face? But she cannot stay here, she must go on. She reaches out farther, farther.

She feels something.

The conduit for the pneumatic-tube system.

Yes!

She can write a message and stuff it into the capsule and send it *swoosh* to the newspaper room. The capsule will slam into the terminus with a bang that would wake the dead. Wally will hear it, surely he'll open it and read her message—

But she doesn't know where she is.

Don't panic.

She feels her way in the darkness along the tube line to the terminal. Her fingers move along the small desk top for a paper and pencil. But she doesn't know where she is! And she can't see to push the proper button to send the message to the newspaper room in the darkness.

She listens, quietly.

Not a sound.

He can't find her in the darkness.

But she can't wait here forever!

She feels along the wall, finds the light switch, flips it on. Blinks in the sudden light. Looks around. She is alone. Quickly, quickly, she writes on the paper the number of the pneumatic-tube station, giving her location. Stuffs the paper into the capsule.

She slips the capsule into the tube, fingers fumbling, can't manage the clasp, can't get it shut—quickly, before he comes!

There! Shut!

She pushes the button and the capsule is sucked out and down the lines of hollow tubing. No stopping it now! With a loud *whoosh* it disappears.

And with two sudden loud footsteps the man appears around the stacks behind her.

She whirls, screams—and then sees who it is. Instead of running for her life she collapses, falls gratefully against him.

"Peter," she sobs. "Thank God it's you!"

He holds her tightly.

"He's up there," she says, pointing up the aisle. "The maniac! He's after me! I heard his footsteps up there!"

"No," he says gently, in his lovely soft Charles Laughton voice. "No, my dear, you are mistaken. He is not up there."

She stares in bewilderment, in horror, up at him. And she understands.

She screams as his hands reach her throat.

The capsule shoots through the pneumatic-tube system and in seconds slams noisily to rest in its container in the empty newspaper room.

Wally is upstairs in the catalog department, looking for Katie. He sees no one. No guards, no maniacs, no one.

It is spooky, but nothing is out of order. It is quiet here in the public section of the library.

He does not know how to find his way into the stacks.

The walls are thick and solid, hard stone. They muffle any sound.

He closes his eyes, tries to sense danger. He opens his eyes. Everything looks ordinary.

His best bet, he decides, is to return to the newspaper room and wait to hear from her.

He's becoming an old maid, he decides, worrying this way.

His fingers are around her throat, and he understands why Peter loves her. She is soft and beautiful, warm and alive, she is Peter's contact with life.

We are all locked alone in our skins, caught inside, sealed off from all contact with the rest of the world. Unless we can reach out and, through love, touch another human soul.

The most blessed gift of all, the gift of not being alone in the universe. That is what she has given Peter.

His fingers close more tightly around her throat, and he smiles. He understands how Peter will feel tomorrow, when he finds out. His only contact will be gone. He too will be alone.

And then perhaps he will be free.

For years he has tried to get out; Peter would not let him. Finally, five years ago, he escaped for the first time. And then it had taken him nearly a year to get out again. But since then it was becoming easier; Peter was getting weaker. He had got out in Hyannis and again in Atlanta and again just two weeks ago and since then he was emerging almost at will. Perhaps with Katie dead Peter would finally give up.

And he would be free for all time.

He doesn't even notice Katie's fingers scratching at

his hands. His own fingers squeeze tighter.

Wally stands in the newspaper room, looking around. He knows this feeling he has for her is distorting his judgment. And Madame Szilardi telephoning all the time doesn't help, and finding out that Peter was in Atlanta when a girl was murdered, was at Hyannis when a girl was killed—all that does not help calm him down.

And yet, what is there to be upset about?

He looks around the room.

Why does he feel something is wrong? Is he becoming a nut like Madame Szilardi? But damn it, something here is *different*. Something has subliminally changed. . . .

He looks carefully around the room. The piles of microfiche newspapers, surely they're all just as they were when he left them. The notes he has been making. The telephone in the corner. The pneumatic-tube system. The lamp by the . . .

He stops.

He turns back to the pneumatic-tube system. Was there a capsule in it before? He walks over to it, opens the capsule, and finds a crumpled piece of paper: "HELP! K 34"

He runs out into the hallway and shouts. Where is that damned guard? He looks again at the note. The number must indicate where she is in the stacks, but he doesn't know where the hell K 34 is.

He yells again. Where is the guard? Where is everyone?!

The long empty halls echo his cries for help, the reverberations die away, and he is still standing there, alone and lost.

And helpless.

Fingers around her throat, cutting off her breath. Gasping, grasping for it—the fingers too tight. Bright, swirling colors. Spinning aisles of books. Blackness, then the colors again. Fingers around her throat.

She has perhaps thirty seconds of consciousness left. Instead of panic, a calm descends. Her mind clears of terror. Find something. Do something. Only seconds left now, only one chance to do—what?

Her arms are dangling down behind her. Her hands flail across the pneumatic-receptacle table. Her fingers, scrambling with a life of their own, close instinctively around the pencil she had used to write her note. Without thinking, her mind already descending from the colors into gray darkness, the fingers clutch the pencil like a knife, her arm with one last grasp at life lifts the fingers and she thrusts upward with all her force into his groin.

For one moment there is no reaction. She thinks she has failed, she is resigned to death, and then the fingers around her throat fall away. He staggers back, releasing her completely, he doubles over in pain.

Her legs have no strength. As he releases her she falls to the floor.

She sees that he has fallen too. He is on his knees. He retches. Then she sees his eyes clearing again, the pain fading.

She struggles to her feet and backs away down the aisle. She tries to scream, to call out, but her battered throat will not respond. It is all she can do to breathe; to shout is out of the question.

She staggers away from him, down the aisle.

And now he is on his feet too, and coming after her.

* * *

On the third floor Wally finds the guard emerging from the men's room, zipping his pants.

"Hey, what's all the noise?"

Wally shoves the note in his face. The guard takes one look and leads Wally around the corner. "It'll be faster this way. We can go down these stairs and enter the stacks through the science section. That'll be close to where she is."

They run down the stairs.

The blackness falls around her as she finds the light switch and throws it. He can't see her in the dark. The light switches are not easy to find, impossible for him to locate in the darkness. She runs down the aisle as fast as she can, hands tracing her path along the towering stacks of books.

She hears him stumble after her, following the sound of her footsteps, doggedly on her trail, until finally he takes a wrong turn around one corner of the nine-foot-high stacks of books, and she is safe.

For the moment.

"Katie," he calls. "Please, Katie, come to me. You know you must die here tonight, my love."

She is frozen, two aisles away from him, unable to move for fear of making a sound. If she could make it to the stairs, if she could get to a different floor, then through the door—but if she moves he will hear her.

And meanwhile he is moving. Slowly, listening for her, he is searching in the darkness.

But he will never find her—

And suddenly a cold light shines out, filling the stacks with white horror. He has stumbled on the Xerox machine, he has punched the button and pulled back the top cover and it is flipping away automatically, maniacally, throwing its horrible white light out into the stacks, flooding the books and the aisles and Peter and Katie with its cold desolate glow.

He sees her. There is nowhere left to hide.

He comes down the aisle after her.

In desperation she turns and climbs up the bookshelf, pulls herself up to the top of the nine-foot stack.

He stands at the bottom, looks up at her, smiles. He shakes his head. He reaches up for her.

"Katie!"

Wally's voice!

She screams, the sound desperately rasping out of her bruised throat.

Footsteps, running toward them!

"Here!" she screams again. *"Wally, I'm here!"*

With a roar of rage he jumps up after her, catches her ankle. She pulls away. He scrambles up onto the stack, she falls back across it, kicking, he loses his grip, reaches out wildly, catches hold of the uppermost shelf—and the stack of books tips over.

Wally comes flying around the corner of the aisle as twelve hundred pounds of books and wooden racks comes plummeting down on Peter's head, with another hundred and fifteen pounds of Katie on top of them. The books are ancient heavy volumes, and there is an avalanche of them, and in the sudden silence that follows their fall there is no movement.

And then Katie crawls to her feet. Wally, holding his gun in his right hand, hurries to her and helps her down from the mound of books and crashed shelving. Beneath the mound, Peter lies still.

One leg is sticking out from under the heavy pile of books, protruding at an unnatural angle. His nose is smashed, he seems to be coated with blood. His eyes open and he asks softly, "Did he hurt you, Katie? Are you—"

"Peter," she says.

Wally is holding her.

"It's Peter," she says to Wally, still not understanding, not believing.

Wally nods. "He killed a girl in Atlanta, and another in Hyannis. He murdered a girl in a motel here just two weeks ago."

"No," Peter says. "Not me. I didn't—"

And then his eyes glaze over, and quickly they clear again. And he chuckles. "Of course he did it," Charles Laughton says. "Don't let him talk you out of it. And we very nearly got you tonight, didn't we, love?" he says to Katie. "Very, very nearly. Just the slightest of slips 'tween the cup and the lips, eh?" He chuckles again, building up to a rasping laugh. "Don't you get it? Don't you get the joke? It is, after all, on you, my love."

"He's out of his mind," Wally says, trying to comfort her.

"Don't you believe it," he rasps. "I'm as sane as Peter is. None of it was of my doing, I was only trying to get out. It's your fault," he says to Katie. "You wouldn't let him alone—"

"That's not true," Peter says, breaking through. "Don't listen to him. I was too weak, I couldn't keep him—"

"What does he know?" Charles Laughton continues without even a breath. "He knows nothing. And *you* know nothing. You think you've won? Do you think that?"

He laughs.

"Because I'm helpless now? Because my leg is twisted under me? Idiot! Don't you understand? Don't you realize what has happened? I'm *here*, talking to you, *and he can't stop me*! I've won! I'm free! It's Peter who's lost now. I'm in control. He'll never get back in!

"So what will happen now? Shall I tell you? Will they execute me for those murders I committed? Yes," he says to Wally, "I committed them. And two others besides. But they won't execute me, they won't even send me to jail. They'll say Peter did them, and they'll say Peter was sick. They'll send Peter to an institution, to *cure* him."

He laughs, chokes, gasps.

"Oh dear," he says. "Isn't life funny? Perhaps I'll let Peter out again for just a little bit, so they will think that finally he is cured. So they will release him. Would you like that, Katie? Would you like to have your Peter back again, Katie?

"I don't think you would. Because when they finally do release him, we will come—he and I—to you. And then Peter will fall back inside and watch helplessly while I kill you. Eventually, finally, Katie, I will come back and kill you."

Wally's hand, holding the gun, rises.

It comes down to this, he tells himself. The whole universe collapses into this one point in time, here and now. Because he's right, Peter or whatever it is that's inside him, he knows what will happen. He should be put in jail for life, he should be executed. But there's no court in this country that will convict him. The murdering bastard is legally innocent by reason of insanity and they'll put him in a hospital and he'll fool them and come out again—

His arm straightens, the gun at the end of it is clutched tightly and not wavering, pointing at the grinning face half-buried in the pile of books. Katie doesn't see it, she is between Wally and Peter, staring in transfixed horror at Peter.

Wally's left hand comes up, grips the gun handle, steadies it. His right forefinger tightens on the trigger.

His hands hold tight, stretched out in front of him. But the gun begins to shake.

He has to die, Wally tells himself.

He *wants* to die. He can't live like that. He isn't begging, he's looking right at me. But deep in Peter's eyes Wally sees a bright, silently screaming light.

The gun is shaking. Wally squeezes it hard, trying to keep it still.

This is where I make my decision. We can't go on like this, we can't let the animals take over. But Peter's eyes are not animal eyes. There is a beast in there with Peter, but Peter himself is in there too.

Wally can't hold the gun steady.

He tries to squeeze the trigger, he tries to dredge up all the arguments, all the reasons.

He can't. He simply can't do it.

He releases his grip on the gun. It falls to the floor.

Katie jumps. "What—?" She sees the gun lying there. She sees the tortured doubt in his face. She throws herself against him, holding him, hugging him.

They turn away from Peter, walk up the aisle, lean against a bookshelf. "Oh, God," Wally says. "My hands are still shaking." He holds them out to show her. She grips them tightly.

"I used to think, if we could all just get tough," he says, "if we only had the guts to point the gun and pull the trigger, we could blow them all away. I thought that was the answer. I mean, Christ, the courts don't work, the jails don't work, *something* has to work."

She puts her arms around him, her face against his chest.

"They're still out there," he says.

"Who?"

"All of them. All the other Peters. Destroying the city the way the Goths sacked Rome. The enemy." He pauses. "I *wanted* to kill him."

"I know."

"I *could* have killed him."

"No, you couldn't."

"Why not? Why can't we just kill them all the way they try to kill us?"

"Because then it would be like Pogo's nightmare: *We have seen the enemy and they are us.*"

He laughs, and his diaphragm muscles suddenly relax and the laugh dies into a long sigh as the bottled-up air inside his chest spills out. He breathes deeply, slowly. He lightly touches her neck, gently tracing the ugly, lurid welts now deepening there.

"It's not easy, is it?" he asks.

She looks up at him, shakes her head. "It was never supposed to be," she says.

EPILOGUE

Peter is now incarcerated at Mill Valley State Hospital, classified as an acute schizophrenic. Three weeks ago he lapsed into a catatonic state. The prognosis is uncertain.

Wally passed the lieutenant's examination shortly after Christmas. He is currently assigned as county liaison officer with the INS. He has been granted a year's leave of absence, beginning this September, to study for a master's degree at Rutgers in criminal justice.

Katie is still working at the public library. She was offered a job as head librarian of the city library in Ithaca, but turned it down. Next year she will commute from Rutgers.

Madame Szilardi accompanied Wally and Katie back to Ohio for the wedding last May, then returned immediately to New York. She remembers vividly the terrible emanations she felt from Peter when they first met, and berates herself for not paying more attention to them.

And the enemy is still out there.

Bestselling Books for Today's Reader

Bestselling Books

☐ 16663-3 **DRAGON STAR** Olivia O'Neill $2.95

☐ 08950-X **THE BUTCHER'S BOY** Thomas Perry $2.95

☐ 55258-7 **THE MYRMIDON PROJECT** Chuck Scarborough & William Murray $3.25

☐ 65366-9 **THE PARTRIACH** Chaim Bermant $3.25

☐ 70885-4 **REBEL IN HIS ARMS** Francine Rivers $3.50

☐ 78374-0 **STARSTRUCK** Linda Palmer $3.25

☐ 02572-2 **APOCALYPSE BRIGADE** Alfred Coppel $3.50

☐ 65219-0 **PASSAGE TO GLORY** Robin Leigh Smith $3.50

☐ 75887-8 **SENSEI** David Charney $3.50

☐ 05285-1 **BED REST** Rita Kashner $3.25

☐ 62674-2 **ON ANY GIVEN SUNDAY** Ben Elisco $3.25

☐ 75700-6 **SEASON OF THE STRANGLER** Madison Jones $2.95

☐ 28929-0 **THE GIRLS IN THE NEWSROOM** Marjorie Margolis $3.50